Coming to Terms

Warren Carrier

BOOKS BY WARREN CARRIER

Novels

The Hunt
Bay of the Damned
Death of a Chancellor
An Honorable Spy
Murder at the Strawberry Festival
Death of a Poet
Justice at Christmas

Poetry

The Cost of Love
Toward Monetbello
Leave Your Sugar for the Cold Morning
The Diver
An Ordinary Man
Risking the Wind

Translations

City Stopped in Time

Edited Books

Reading Modern Poetry
Handbook of World Literature
Literature From the World

Coming to Terms

by

Warren Carrier

Panther Creek Press
Spring, Texas

Published by Panther Creek Press
SAN 253-8520
116 Tree Crest
P.O. Box 130233
Panther Creek Station
Spring, Texas 77393-0233

Cover photo © 2001 by Patty Wentz
Portland, Oregon
Cover design by Adam Murphy
The Woodlands, Texas

Manufactured in the United States of America
Printed and bound by Data Duplicators, Inc.
Houston, Texas

1 2 3 4 5 6 7 8 9 10   ·

Library of Congress Cataloguing in Publication Data

Carrier, Warren

    Coming to terms

    I. Title   II. Fiction

ISBN 0-9747839-6-X

for

Judy and Ethan and Greg

Has some Vast Imbecility,
Mighty to build and blend,
But impotent to tend,
Framed us in jest, and left us to hazardry?

Thomas Hardy

1 *JOSÉ VIDA*

There was no food or water in the shed the way there was supposed to be. Mateo had explained that the owner of the shed always left food and water, but they were not to go up to the house because he didn't want to see them, or even know they were there. They could make use of the shed, take what he left there, and then move on north.

José peered over the top of the bushes at the house, then ducked down. A woman was coming out of the house. She got in a car and drove away as he watched through the bushes, pulling them to one side just enough to see. Maybe the man was more interested in the woman than in making sure of the food and water. Lupe needed food and water for the child she carried inside her.

He had so little money left. Mateo had laughed and said the money he had was not even enough to buy two tacos. The rest of his money he had saved he gave to Mateo to help them cross the border without being caught by the border patrol or the *coyotes*.

Mateo had provided a map on which he had marked the path through the mountains and places they could stop and find supplies.

If there was food and water in the house, maybe he could get them himself. He didn't want to be a thief. He didn't want his son to have a thief for a father. He had refused to carry drugs the way some illegals did. He waited, not moving, then he decided to check on Lupe again. He worked his way down the slope to the shed, a one-horse barn with a mattress and a table and two chairs and a calendar that Lupe said was two years old.

Lupe was lying on the mattress on her side, her big belly out in front of her. She looked so strange, that little body, so skinny, and the big belly.

"José," Lupe said. "I am afraid."

"Do not be afraid." He knelt down beside her on the mattress.

"Where is the food and the water?"

"The man must have forgotten. Maybe he was too busy."

"Did you ask him?"

"We are not supposed to ask, remember?"

"But the baby needs food and water. Maybe I should not have come with you in my condition, but I didn't want you to go without me."

"I will go back and ask."

"The time is so close and we still have a long way to go." She crossed herself.

He patted Lupe's hand and got up. He had to get what they needed, no matter what Mateo said.

The slope was so steep that he to use the bushes to pull himself up. The bushes cut his hands. There was a path that circled east and back to the house, but he didn't want to be seen. He stopped at the edge of the cleared space where the house stood. There was no sound except the wind and the birds. He walked slowly to the house.

He tried to look in a window but the shutters were closed on the inside. He went to the door and waited, listening. After a while he knocked gently on the door. He knocked more loudly. Still nothing. He walked around the house and found that all the windows were shuttered and closed. He tried the garage door, but it was locked. He circled the house to the front door and knocked again. He tried the knob. It turned.

If he could find some food and a container to get some water, that's all he would take. He pulled the door, waited and looked in. It was dark, and the contrast with the bright morning sunlight made it difficult to see anything at all. He stood in the door and waited for his eyes to grow accustomed to the darkness. Furniture. Then he saw the chair with the man sitting in it.

"Good morning," he said in English. He had practiced his English, the little he knew, but his voice trembled.

The man did not reply. He smelled it. The smell of death. He had smelled it in Mexico in his village when someone died. He saw the gun lying on the floor and blood on the man's shirt and on the floor. He walked slowly to the man and touched him. He was cool. There was a hole in his skull. He crossed himself. If he were caught here, the police might think he was a terrorist because he was an illegal.

The big room was open to a kitchen. He walked carefully to the kitchen and opened the refrigerator. There was a carton of milk that smelled sweet and a half a loaf of bread and a small block of cheese. He collected them quickly and walked to the door. He pushed the door closed behind him with his back, walked to the edge of the yard and began his descent to the shed, sliding and almost falling.

The woman must have seen the dead man. Maybe she went for the police. Why would man with a house kill himself? In his mind he crossed himself. They would leave quickly and continue north. The dead man would have given him the food he had taken, if he had been alive. May God forgive him, he said softly. And forgive me for taking the food.

At last he had food for Lupe. And his son.

2 *LAURIE NEWTON*

As she stood beside her father she felt as though she were standing outside herself. They faced the mahogany coffin in the "chapel" of the crematorium. There was no priest, no altar, unless that little table was meant to resemble one. There was a small stained glass window at the rear. A pyre they wouldn't see would turn Mark into ashes like a Hindu. The ashes, according to his wish, as reported by Leah, to be scattered over the ocean somewhere.

She hadn't known him very well. She knew his face as though it were that of a distant relative. What she knew about him was a kind of myth, stories she heard and didn't know if they were true. They had no connections, except for one long ago she preferred to forget. And that now seemed a kind of myth.

Jimmy, hunched slightly as thought to listen carefully to a client, stood beside Father. Even though Jimmy was closer in age to Mark, she thought he had not known him better than she. They had certainly not been friendly toward each other. Father, slump shouldered, seemed beaten down by the emotional trauma he had been put through. Had actually Mark done it hoping it would affect Father this way? Mark had fended them all off. You'll feel guilty, Tom had said before she left, offering free the trite noodles of wisdom he purchased from his analyst.

She refused to feel guilty. Mark had chosen to do what he did. She had no part in it. When she was young she had looked up to him as a little sister would. And, after Iraq, he had become even more alienated. The army had wanted to drape a flag.

The unctuous, formally attired director of the crematorium appeared like a ghost from behind the drapes at the side and spoke in a whisper to her father. Whom would he disturb if he spoke aloud? Half a dozen people stood beside them, only one of whom she had even heard of. Jimmy had told her under his breath that that was Leah, a friend of Mark's.

Her father nodded to the director, wiped his eyes on the back of his hand, and she saw, to her astonishment, that the coffin was gliding to the left on a automatic track of some sort. The track was taking Mark directly into the furnace.

She heard a soft gasp from Leah behind her. They were all agoggle now. Stiffled hysteria at the grotesqueness of the scene? The drapes fell back like those of a stage at the end of a play.

Her father nodded again, turning to them at last. She stumbled from the room and found herself loose in a clump of strangers, sun-blinded, on the tarmac of a parking lot.

"You all right?" Jimmy had his hand on her elbow.

"It's just that it's all so…" She left her sentence unfinished.

"I know," Jimmy said. He turned to father. "Should we go someplace for lunch?"

Father looked surprised. He nodded and blew his nose on a tissue. "Perhaps we should ask Leah." He had always been inclusive. He adopted lost sheep among his students at Berkeley and brought them home for dinner.

Jimmy appeared annoyed, but turned to Leah, trailing uncertainly behind them toward her car. "Would you care to join us for lunch?"

Her face a sketch of reluctance, she nodded abruptly.

Other mourners - colleagues from UCSD? - scattered to their cars. Father rushed toward them, hair flying in the breeze, and shook their hands. Two of them looked like veterans.

"Do you know a place nearby?" Jimmy said to Leah. "I think none of us knows this part of San Diego very well."

They were watching Father.

"There's an Italian restaurant in La Mesa, just off the freeway. You can follow me." Her clothes, a dark suit of light weight wool, looked expensive, but hung loosely on her as though it were bought on sale and not for fit. She wore flat sandals. Her black hair was unkempt. She wore no discernable makeup over her dark skin.

Jimmy agreed. They went silently to their cars.

The restaurant was a converted bank, Leah informed them with an ironic smile. Laurie found herself watching the patrons to distract herself. There were business types in shirts and ties; a family with young and noisy children; a single woman eating by herself and receiving special attention from the padrone. The scurrying waitresses were daughters of the *padrone*, Leah remarked.

The food was good. She was surprised at how hungry she was. Leah had half a bottle of wine.

Father asked Jimmy about his daughter Linda. Jimmy said she was doing well at Mills College. He did not ask about Marie, since Jimmy and Marie had gotten a divorce. He asked about her husband. Tom was trying to make a go of it in publishing. He was romantic about books, but he was doing well in a bad stock market where he was hard-headed. She did not tell him Tom was becoming something of a bore. She had a feeling her father wanted grandchildren.

Father asked about the location of Mark's cabin. It was above Alpine, Leah said. It had escaped the fires. Father thought they ought to close it up, or whatever it was that needed to be done. Jimmy asked Leah if Mark had made a will.

Leah said he had. She thought it was in the old steel filing cabinet in the garage.

"Do you know the contents?" Jimmy said.

"He got one of those kits from a bookstore, filled it out, and had some people in the computer center witness it. He told me he was leaving his stereo equipment to me and the house to Laurie."

"Oh," she heard herself say, dumbfounded. Why did he do that? She had no use for a cabin in the parched hills above Alpine. She had her inheritance from her mother, enough now, after Tom had invested it, to keep her from want, even without all of Tom's money.

"I suppose we should retrieve the will then, too."

"I thought the house was sealed by the sheriff," Leah said.

Father turned to Jimmy for legal counsel.

11

"Once the coroner has ruled it was death by suicide, the seal is released," Jimmy said. He shrugged dismissively.

"He named you executor," Leah said to Jimmy.

"I guess we had better go to Alpine," Jimmy said, clearly annoyed again. "Can you take us to the house? I'll need to find the will. It may be valid. It'll need to go through probate. The stereo equipment probably shouldn't be left for prowlers to find. If I'm the executor, I guess I can anticipate the court and place it in your custody until it's all settled."

An expression of uncertainty took possession of Leah's face. She glanced at her watch and then at the wall. "I took the day off from work, and I'm living with a friend who..." She broke off and ran her hand through her untamed hair. "Okay," she said. She clearly had no desire to be in their company.

Leah was older than she had guessed at first. When she talked she appeared younger, but when she was stayed silent, she seemed to age. She must have shared Mark's bitter views.

They decided to go in one car and drop Leah off at her car on the way back. Leah sat in front with Jimmy to provide directions.

Laurie sat in back with her father who sank deep into his seat and closed his eyes. She was shocked to see him look so old, and so defeated. She held his hand.

3 *MICHAEL HORNE*

He had been sitting in the air-conditioned, refurbished old Victorian he had leased for the year, watching a black kid, music clamped to his ears, pump home from school on his bike over the scabbed street. A cat slept under his neighbor's rusty car. Handel on his portable stereo, sipping a cold Boddingtons ale, he had been reading snippets of material for his paper. The phone rang.

"It's Leah Stein," the voice said.

Mark's friend. She had never called him before.

"Has something happened to Mark?"

"He's had an accident."

"Is he okay?" He waited, apprehension rising.

"He's dead." She said it abruptly, and stopped.

He felt the shock and reached deep to find his breath. "What happened?" he said, after a moment. He felt suspended.

"He shot himself." This time she sucked in her breath and let it out in a burst. She was crying.

"Accidentally?"

"He committed suicide." He could barely hear her.

He expected her to say it. There were tears running down his cheeks. He could see Mark's bitter face.

"Dr. Horne?" Leah voice was hoarse.

13

"When?"

"Last night, they say. I found him this morning. We had planned to go to Borrego Springs. I came by and..." She broke off.

He felt numb.

"You'd better come."

"Yes," he said.

"If you let me know when your plane will be arriving, I'll pick you at the airport."

"Thank you. Where is he?"

"The county morgue. They had to do an autopsy. I've already identified him, but they'll want you to do it officially. I told them I'd call you. I'd better leave you my number."

Tears were sliding down his nose.

It was the same feeling he had had at Janice's death when Mark's anger at her dying turned against him. Was a natural death someone's fault? A blood vessel breaks and spills its cargo, pulse after pulse, into gray matter. We died one way or another. Were we responsible for each other's deaths? Did blaming someone assuage grief?

He had to call Jimmy and Laurie. Neither had been close to Mark, but he was their brother. He had to make his plane reservations. He should let the director of the Institute know. He blew his nose. He got out the phone book to look up his travel agent's number.

His voice was clogged and he had to clear it. Jimmy was ten minutes coming out of his conference. He was calm at the news. He would meet his father in San Diego. He would stay at the Westgate where he usually stayed on business trips. He would make reservations there for all three of them.

He called Laurie's house in Connecticut and the brownstone in New York and got answering machines in both places. He left a message with the bare facts and said Jimmy was making reservations at the Westgate.

The cleaning woman would have to be notified. He had to pack and drive to Hobby whenever his travel agent secured a flight for him. He gazed absently out to the street again, waiting for the agent's call. His neighbor started up his rusty car. The cat scampered.

The flight, the identification of the body, the coroner's inquest, the cremation - he had drifted through it all like a sleepwalker. He drowsed as they climbed toward Alpine. The sound of the car took him back to traveling at night in the back seat of his father's car. Enclosed in his mind, he watched flares of the past floating by like galactic debris.

His family had scattered beyond him: Janice flown to her spirit world; Mark burned to a box of ashes; Jimmy divorced, submerged in corporate law; Laurie married into east coast gentility. At Janice's funeral, that last gathering, busy with a miscellany of Janice's family, friends, colleagues, the unforgettably scene: Mark's arms chopping the air, his words confused and wild, faces frozen around them. Had her death deranged him? Except for his strange bond to his mother, Mark had chosen not to belong.

The car slowed and turned off the highway onto gravel. Bumps and dust, yuccas, the smell of sage.

"Here," Leah said. "At that tree."

And now on a dirt road that climbed steeply through brush, they swerved and slowed to low gear and came out at the top of a knoll. The site overlooked canyons and smoky mountains. It was like all desert mountain backlands, arid, dotted sparsely with scrubby trees and low bushes. The house was a rectangular adobe with a red tile roof. A pole at the edge of the clearing looped wires to the eaves. A boulder crouched beside the door.

"My God," Jimmy said. "This place is really remote. Does it have water?"

"A well. Water is brought to the house by an electric pump. There's a septic tank."

Leah leading the way, they crunched over gravelly dirt to the house. The sheriff's yellow seal was still on the door.

"The sheriff is in no hurry to come all the way out here just to remove his notice." Jimmy said. "Do you have a key?"

"There's one over the window." Leah stood on tiptoe and drew a key from a crack in the adobe. She hesitated, then handed the key to Jimmy.

The interior of the house was dark, with narrows strips of light entering between the louvers of the shutters. Leah went to the windows and opened the shutters while they waited. She turned on a lamp and looked toward the chair beside a south window. There were dark stains on the chair and on the Mexican rug in front of the chair. Tears welled up and he looked away. A chain of cells, replicating from the beginning of biological time: his son.

4 *JIMMY HORNE*

He was irritated that Mark had named him executor. He glanced at the bloody chair and rug again. An ugly way to do it. Potential suicides didn't concern themselves about the mess somebody would have to clean up. As a reservist, Mark had been taken from his job at UCSD and sent to Iraq. He had been wounded, but he had survived and returned to his computers. Given the job market, he was lucky.

While he did not hold academic rank, he claimed to be a genius with the machines that most of the faculty he worked for knew little about. And he had this crumby retreat remote from civilization and its discontents. But he had no wife, or any family he was willing to acknowledge. The digital sounds of jazz were not enough. Flaky Leah was not enough.

"Where's the filing cabinet you mentioned?" he said to Leah.

"In the garage." Leah put her words into an awkward rush to the kitchen. A lizard skittered across the wall behind her.

He followed as she fumbled with the door from the kitchen into the garage. A naked bulb came on and a green cabinet covered with dusty boxes came into view. Beyond was an ancient Volvo.

The cabinet doors were locked. He unhooked a tiny Swiss knife his key chair. Leah smiled when she saw it, no doubt surprised that

17

he would carry a knife, or try to break into a locked file. He worked the knife into the opening. It gave suddenly and Leah laughed.

The files were old but arranged in alphabetical order. He found a folder tabbed Will and pulled it. It did seem to contain a will. They returned to the living room.

"Let's sit down somewhere."

They avoided the end of the room with the bloody chair.

"Are you going to do a formal reading?" Laurie said. She was obviously upset at the probable confirmation of Leah's report that she had been given the house. She sat cross-legged on the tile floor.

"I'm just checking. This is not a formal reading."

The will was a printed form with fill-ins. He searched first for witness signatures. There were three, notarized. It appeared to be in order. In lieu of anything else, it would probably pass muster.

It disposed of the property essentially as Leah had said it did: house to Laurie; stereo and records to Leah; Volvo to one María Gomez, cleaning woman; books, papers and prints to Father. He was himself named executor. If Father or Laurie died before the will took effect, he was to receive their shares of the estate.

"What am I going to do with this house?" Laurie said. "I don't want it. Why did he do this? There's probably a mortgage on it anyway."

"There's no mortgage." Leah said. "He bought it outright about ten years ago and fixed it up."

Laurie's face was an etching of distress. She and Tom owned at least three houses, each one of them worth twenty times more than this one: a country house in Connecticut, surrounded by trees, a mile from the Sound where kept a small sailing yacht they had taken him on once; a brownstone in Manhattan; a villa in Aruba he had seen photographs of. What she would do with this shack was a good question. She could sell it. In the crazy California housing market, it was probably worth three hundred thousand. He would search for the deed.

They fell into a constrained silence. Father reconnoitered the prints on the wall. What had possessed the old guy at this point in his life he would take leave from Berkeley to go to Texas to write about scientific ethics? A waste of time to try to educate his colleagues, citing theories few of his fellow scientists knew enough about to take into account, or that ordinary citizens would find acceptable. Father had always cared more about being right than in being sensible.

Even though Mark had been their mother's favorite (she would have denied it), it was Father whom Mark resembled more. They had the same fractious attitude toward establishments. He wondered what Mark had done with his inheritance from Mother. Very likely he had used some of it to buy this house and fix it up. He had expensive stereo gear. The computer and printer didn't seem all that special, but, of course, he had access to the computers at UCSD. If there were significant money in the bank, or investments, he would have mentioned them in his will. The Miró prints seemed out of character. Given his paranoia and bitterly resentful attitude toward society and authority, his suicide was entirely in character.

"I'll have to come back for this stereo stuff," Leah said, breaking into the silence. "I don't even know how to take this stuff apart." Her voice cracked. There was more than stereo here.

Laurie stepped to her side and put an arm around her. "I'm sure someone can be found to help you," she said. Her placating words sounded shaky.

Leah shrank from Laurie's embrace. Father seated on the rug-covered sofa, was holding his hands over his face.

Jimmy found himself remembering Mark's disastrous tenth birthday party. When Mother announced that Father's car was ascending the hill in front of the house, there was a moment of giggling as the guests, boys from the neighborhood and the school, waited in anticipation. There was a hush as Father opened the door and when Mark entered they all shouted from the dining room: Surprise!

Mark backed away. "I don't want a party," he shouted, and ran upstairs to the bedroom they shared. Father followed, but Mark had slammed the door and locked it. They could hear Mark yelling: "I don't want a party! I don't want a party!"

Nothing Mark had ever done, or that people had tried to do for him, had seemed to be something he wanted, or could accept. He rejected the world he had to live in, and he ended his odds with his life in a lonely shanty in these wild, charred mountains.

5 *LEAH STEIN*

She was embarrassed to have broken down in front of strangers. Mark's father had taken them to dinner. His brother, Jimmy, had invited them for a drink and interrogated her about herself as though she were a hostile witness until Mark made him stop.

Mark disliked all of them. Yet, she thought, for some unfathomable reason he had wanted his father's approval.

She had longed to be accepted by her own father, even though she hated him. She had wanted her ex-husband to recognize she was a person, not a thing to be used, discarded, then admitted back into his graces when it pleased him. And now he was in jail for making ecstasy in his garage.

She chose not to dwell on futility. Mark had been a friend. Now he was dead. Lydia was her friend. Now she was dying. She sat in Mark's computer chair. They were all intruders into Mark's life.

"There's nothing more to do here, is there?" Jimmy said. He dealt with them as though they were clients. Under his arrogant, aristocratic profile lay a moral vacuum. If I can come back in another life, Lydia had said bitterly, I want to come back as a tall white male. Jimmy lived exclusively in a corrupt world. He had to be loaded now, with his inheritance from his mother and high fees.

"I have no need to stay longer," Laurie said. "But what am I

20

going to do with this damned house?" High cheeks and hollows, she stood akimbo in her black silk suit, eyes fixed on Jimmy.

Jimmy shrugged. "Sell it."

"I'll buy it from you," her father said. He looked exhausted. At least he cared. Jimmy and Laurie acted put upon. "I don't know what I'll do with it, but if you don't want it, I'll buy it."

"Not the best investment," Jimmy said. He obviously didn't understand his father. His well-heeled clients would buy something, roll it over, and make money. What else was there in this world? "We can have it appraised."

"You can have it, Daddy," Laurie said. She was trying to understand her father's feelings. Why would he want it?

Maybe she should offer to buy it from Laurie. Or Dr. Horne.

"Easy to do," Jimmy said. "You can simply sign it over."

It was all the same to Jimmy. Houses, real estate appraisals, wills, books, people, his brother's ashes.

"What do you wanted to do about the stereo?" Jimmy was addressing her.

"I don't know how to deal with it, and it's too much to carry in my lap." The thought of coming back alone to the house was frightening.

"She can come back and get it," Laurie said. "She has a key. She can bring someone who knows how to disconnect and reconnect these things."

"Okay," Jimmy said. "Probably Father ought to take the prints. Anything else we need to settle right now?"

"Are we taking too much of your time?" Laurie said.

"Mark's dead, and by his own choice. We're trying to tie up all the loose ends he left for us. I've got things to do, clients whose appointments I have postponed. Father has his obligations in Texas. I have no idea what you do, if anything, but I doubt you can do it out here on the reservation." Jimmy looked cold and angry.

"You son of a bitch. Don't you condescend to me like that. And Mark was not just some minor client of yours."

"I left my business to come down here for a funeral, if that's what it was, and I have been given the job of executor without being asked, and I will do it. What more do you expect of me? Hang around indefinitely and mope over a brother who didn't give a damn about us, and who, in fact, treated us like dirt?"

"Please," Dr. Horne said. He was clearly distressed.

Laurie went to her father and put her arm around him.

"I'm sorry," Jimmy said.

There was pain in Dr. Horne's face. He turned to her. "I'll help you with your stereo. If you will ride back with my son and daughter to the restaurant parking lot for your car, and drive back here in your own car, I'll help you with the equipment and the CDs. Then you can drive me to my hotel, if you will. Is that okay?"

"Leave you by yourself?" Laurie said.

"I've been by myself since your mother died," Dr. Horne said. He was looking at her questioningly over Laurie's shoulder.

"It's all right with me," she said. She really wanted to be rid of them all.

"All right," Dr. Horne said. "That's the plan."

"I should stay here, too," Laurie said.

"He didn't ask you to," Jimmy said.

"I'd like to be by myself, Laurie," Dr. Horne said. "I'll be fine. Leah will take me to my hotel after we pack the stereo. We'll be in touch."

Laurie looked stricken. She was being dismissed. Jimmy appeared pleased at his father's crispness. The old man hugged Laurie. She kissed him on the cheek, still miffed. Jimmy shook his hand. Dr. Horne turned to Leah. "I'll be here when you get back."

She stood and he shook her hand formally. He looked like he needed a drink. She needed a drink. Mark, tall and skinny, pale faced, had not resembled his father at all. With his high forehead and thicket of hair, Dr. Horne resembled an old fashioned *paterfamilias* in a musty painting.

She got into the back seat of Jimmy's rental BMW.

Mark's face exploded in her brain. His mouth open, his eyes staring at eternity, the smell, the hole in his head, the blood, the bits... She had fallen to her knees before him to plead that it not be so. She had run through the house, sobbing, yelling. The sheriff had required her to meet them at the Interstate turnoff. They followed her to the house, hauled him away in a bag. The questions. What did these fucking civilized people know about that?

She rode down the mountain in the company of strangers.

6 VANESSA PARSONS

After three days, she had turned up zilch. Mark's assistant had tried every trick he knew to make the computer reveal where it was. If your document is there, Hans said, only Mark can find it. A macabre Hans joke. Mark had worked with her on her project. She thought he helped her more than others because he liked her. Had he turned on her and erased it? Had he hidden it somewhere for some reason? Or for no reason? He had committed suicide. Did that mean he had gone off his rocker and knocked out a bunch of documents, and their innocent authors along the way?

If she couldn't find it, it meant three years down the toilet. Her advisor had seen a printout of the first two chapters and approved them, but that was all she had printed out. She should have known it was safer to print everything, no matter how rough, as she went along; but she was a habitual reviser, moving pages and paragraphs, adding, revising, deleting.

Except for the first two chapters in original draft, the whole thing was gone. She had scattered notes, but her fellowship was about to run out. It would take a year to reconstruct her dissertation.

Maybe there would be something at his abode hacienda in the mountains. He had invited her to his house to hear old jazz records, blues from the thirties and forties. She was not that hot for oldies. She knew something about them because her father played tenor sax in a band off and on - when he wasn't playing Baptist preacher, or operating some other kind of scam. When Mark heard about her father, he had invited her to hear his records.

It had been a strange afternoon. She had supposed at first he wanted to seduce her to the strains of "Mood Indigo," the price for his help on the big computer. She was prepared to pay. A lot of academic types wanted to fuck you, one way or another. But Mark had been sincere. Or shy.

An odd guy, a little mad, a political radical, a casualty from Iraq, a whiz on the computer. A son of a bitch who left her in a shit pit.

She contemplated going out to his house. If she could find it. It would probably be locked tight. Maybe she should take Larry with her: he wouldn't mind breaking and entering. Except that she really didn't hanker after his condescending remarks about her being an intellectual. Besides, he had gone off to surf, and nothing would break him away from riding a wave.

She stepped from her long shirt and into a shower to wash off thoughts of Larry and the gloom of her future, letting the hot water flow over her like God's forgiveness. Her ancient Mustang started on the third try. The gas gauge didn't work but she had filled the tank only last week and the only miles she had driven were to the supermarket, the university and the beach.

The temperature gauge was showing red as she reached the top of the grade to Alpine. She stopped at a Shell station and added water. On the freeway again, she watched for the turnoff. She slowed before each exit until she was sure, or at least surer than at the earlier exits, that she had found the right one. When she saw the gnarled tree she was elated: her photographic memory was still working. When the house came into view at the top of the dirt road the Mustang stalled. It started again and struggled on its bald tires through the slippery dirt to the clearing. She got out to the strong smell of sage and hesitated.

The door opened and an old man stood in the entry. For an awful moment she thought Mark had been transformed into to a ghost.

"Hello?"

"Hello," she said shakily. "I'm sorry to bother you. I'm Vanessa Parsons. The man who lived here was helping me with my doctoral dissertation. Now I can't find my file in the computer. It had all my research in it. And I thought..." She was out of breath, having said it so fast. The old guy probably didn't understand a word she said.

"You thought there might be something in the house to help you find it?" The man had a friendly, sad face.

She heard herself breathing easier. "I thought he might have kept notes or data on his computer here."

"Come in. We'll look." He held out his hand. He was taller that he first appeared, wore a thatch of gray-tinged brown hair. "I'm Michael Horne, Mark's father."

"Oh. I'm really sorry about Mark. I didn't mean to intrude."

"It's okay. The computer here looks like a simple word-processor. The computers I'm used to are more elaborate, though my colleagues, I confess, know more than I. One of them is developing a program he calls bioSpice that may do things that now seem unimaginable."

"You're a researcher?"

"A biologist. I'm at Berkeley."

"A professor?" She had not thought of Mark having an academic father.

"You may not be thinking kindly of professors or computer types these days." The lined face became younger in a wry smile. "I was about to make some iced tea. Would you like some? There seems to be nothing stronger around."

"Yes. Can I help?"

He pointed to the computer. "Why don't you get started."

He was not at all like his son who was inevitably coiled tight even when he helped her. Except the time she came to this house and he became awkward. She heard clinking glass from the kitchen. It must difficult to survive a son when it was supposed to be the other way around. He was alone in the house. The funeral had been this morning. Hans had gone. She had thought of going, but she hadn't known him that well. And she was mad at him. She had never gone to a funeral.

There were boxes of discs. It was unlikely that he would put her file on a disc. She flipped through them anyway: program discs, personal files, files with odd names, but no title that would fit her document. She had an eerie sensation as she searched: these were pieces of a dead man's life: a bright, quick, getting older young loner who dressed like a left-over hippie, who had been kind to her for no reason she could fathom.

Had he taken some kind of vengeance like a scorned lover? She booted up the computer and began scanning the menus on the hard drive.

She heard the sound of a car crunching gravel. Horne entered the living room and handed her a glass of iced tea. A car door slammed. A tiny green gecko slithered across the stucco wall behind the computer.

7 LEAH STEIN

There was another car parked in the yard, an old Mustang, as decrepit as her Rabbit. Had someone barged in on Mark's father? In these lonely hills anything could happen.

Dr. Horne greeted her at the door. "There's a grad student from UCSD here. Mark advised her about he dissertation project."

He was holding a glass of iced tea.

A young woman came forward and offered her hand. "I'm Vanessa Parsons," she said. She was black and good-looking. She felt an instant hostility toward her, and struggled to suppress it.

"I'm Leah Stein," she said, shaking the offered hand quickly.

"Vanessa is looking for clues to the program Mark had been helping her put on the computer, and which has apparently been lost," Dr. Horne said. "Would you like some iced tea? I poured this glass for myself but I haven't touched it. If you will take this one, I'll go make myself another."

She accepted the glass. She would have preferred a good stiff vodka on the rocks, but Mark didn't drink and never kept liquor in his house. She would have to wait until she got back to Lydia's house. Vanessa was regarding her curiously. Dr. Horne walked to the kitchen. He had obviously found his way around in her absence. It was his house now.

"Haven't I seen you at the computer center at UCSD" Vanessa said. "You must have visited Mark there."

"Sometimes." How well had Mark known this beauty?

"Have you any ideas what he might have done with my file? Did he store documents somewhere beside the computer center?"

"I wouldn't know anything about it." Her voice was sharper than she should have allowed it to be.

Vanessa shrugged, sat down at the desk that held Mark's computer. The computer was on.

Dr. Horne returned with a glass of tea and rattling ice. "What is the subject of your dissertation?" he asked Vanessa.

Vanessa reacted with surprise. Why would Dr. Horne be interested? "I'm in the lit department. I'm working on a the structures of a selection of novels. More goes on in novels than plot, you know."

"Like what?"

"Archetypes, for one thing. Isn't that what you scientists do? Find order. Or invent it. And make up theories and make things fit?" Her grin revealed even white teeth in her dark face. Another goddamned intellectual.

"Because there's order there," Dr. Horne said. He was smiling back. "In nature as well as in our heads. Order is our way of understanding things. And not arbitrarily, the way novelists compose their novels."

"Novels are more than arbitrary creations. Stories have always fallen into patterns. Of course, some novelists are more aware of structures and have more control of their inventions."

"Like James Joyce?"

Vanessa appeared surprised again. "Right. You must have been exposed to the humanities."

He laughed and turned to her. "I guess novels and science are a long way from counseling unwed mothers."

Was he classifying her? She, too, had had an education and so what? She had read *Ulysses*. Joyce was another dead corpse for the literary coroners. "I live in the real world," she said. It came out hotly against her intention.

"I live in the real world, too," Vanessa said. "My family lives in Watts." Vanessa had seen through to her hostility.

Now she was both angry and embarrassed. Her glass shook in her hand.

Dr. Horne intervened. "Everybody comes from somewhere. And hopes to go somewhere." He turned to Vanessa. Do you know about taking stereo systems apart? Mark left his stereo stuff to Leah and neither one of us knows much about it."

"More than I know about computers. Mark had quite a collection of jazz and blues."

So Vanessa knew about that, too. Well, Mark had said they should live freely. He must have admired her arrogant grace.

"The easiest thing to do is put a certain number of stripes on the wires and give the places they come from the same numbers, then match them when you reassemble," Vanessa said. "What I have is not as good or complex as this system, but that's what I've done when I moved so I wouldn't have to figure it all out again each time. And it seems to me I've moved every year I've been in graduate school."

Vanessa went to the stereo packed wall and moved units out to look behind the cases at the jungle of wires and plugs. Dr. Horne followed.

"I have a pen with red ink. We can mark them with that."

Vanessa and Dr. Horne pulled the tuner and amplifier and disc rotary from the narrow table they rested on. She watched them. Since they were so much smarter, they could do the whole thing. She imitated her clients who waited for everything they had coming before they risked doing anything for themselves.

Once the individual pieces were separated from the system, they began to tote them, wires dangling, to her car.

She opened the trunk and the doors and they began to place the pieces in the trunk, the back seat and the floor.

"Have to leave room for me," Dr. Horne said.

"I can take you back to San Diego, if that's where you're going," Vanessa said.

They piled carousels of discs on the front Passénger seat and floor. One slid out. Birtwhistle. Not a jazz name, was it?

So Vanessa had moved in to offer Dr. Horne a ride. That was all right with her. She didn't want his company anyway.

A wind, heavy with the odor of sage had started up, blowing dust in the yard. She heard a keening sound. She listened. Vanessa stopped with her. Finally, Dr. Horne, fitting the last stack of discs into her car, halted and listened.

"What is that?" he said.

"It's a baby crying," she said.

"Or an animal," Vanessa said.

"I didn't know there were any houses that close."

"There aren't," she said.

Dr. Horne in the lead, they walked to the edge of the yard where the ground broke sharply into a ravine. He pointed. "There's some kind of shed down there."

Another gust of wind carried the sound from the direction of the shed. "There's a path going down from the back of the property," he said. "Did Mark rent out the shed? It isn't big enough for anything much. Maybe a horse."

"Not to my knowledge."

"Perhaps we ought to investigate."

"If there are illegals there, it could be dangerous," she said.

"With a baby?" Vanessa said.

Dr. Horne started down the path.

"Let's all go," Vanessa said.

The path circled back and down through the brush. As they reached the shed the crying became louder. Dr. Horne knocked on the door. The crying stopped.

"Anyone there?" Dr. Horne called.

Was the mother holding something over the baby's mouth to stop the crying? She pushed Dr. Horne aside and opened the door.

"*Somos amigos,*" she said. "*No hay peligro.*"

The woman was sitting on a mattress with her shawl wrapped around the baby. The shawl fell away and the baby began to cry at full pitch. It was recently born, not more than a few hours old.

8 MICHAEL HORNE

It was appalling. The woman had obviously given birth by herself. The place smelled to high heaven. There was no water or sanitary facility in the shed. That the child was alive - and the mother - was a tribute to the determination of the human species to survive.

"Can you speak English?" he said.

The woman regarded him with dark, watchful eyes, and immobile face. The image of a wounded doe he and his grandfather had encountered rose in his memory.

"*¿Hablas inglés?*" Leah said.

The woman shook her head. Her eyes returned to him.

"Ask her if there is anyone with her."

"She may be afraid to answer." But she asked anyway.

The woman hesitated. "*Mi marido.*"

"*¿Dónde está?*"

"*Fué pa buscar comida.*"

"Her husband is with her. He went to look for food."

"Mother and baby need to get to a hospital, or a doctor, at least. The baby is very small. It may be premature, and if it is, it will need special care. The umbilical cord should be taken care of. And whatever else."

"If she goes to a hospital emergency room, which is all she can

31

go to without insurance, they'll send her back to Mexico."

"Then she'll go back with a living child."

"The risk is for her to decide, isn't it?"

"I thought you were a social worker."

"I know how the system works."

Vanessa was watching in what seemed to be a state of shock.

Was he being obtuse? "Let's get them up to the house. At least there is soap and hot water there. They need to be cleaned up. And there must be food in the cupboards. Ask if she is able to walk to the house." The breeze was rising. Birds were flying low in the bushes around them, foraging for insects.

"Of course she's able. She's an Indian peasant, not a middle class Anglo."

Leah explained to the woman what they wanted to do. The woman objected, becoming animated.

Leah translated. The woman was waiting for her husband, José. He would not know where she was. Would they report them to the border patrol?

He asked Leah to assure her that they would not turn them in, and to say that he would watch out for her husband.

The woman was crying softly now. Vanessa took the baby, wrapping her in the shawl, the woman resisting at first. Leah helped the woman rise from the mattress and walk from the shed. He headed a procession along the path to the house. They climbed slowly in the dry heat. Had Mark known about the Mexicans in the shed? Did the Mexicans know that the shack was there for them to use?

The women escorted mother and baby to the bathroom. He could hear bath water running. Vanessa brought out a bundle of clothes to the washer in the kitchen. The infant was crying up a storm. When he went out to the yard to watch for José, he saw that the path to the shed wound father down the ravine. It must have been the path the illegals took to get there. And then he saw a young Mexican man standing at the east end of the clearing.

He beckoned to him. "José?"

"*Sí, señor.*"

"Your wife and the baby are in the house." He pointed and beckoned again. "Everything is all right, okay, *muy bien*. The women are taking care of them." He motioned again and walked toward the door.

José approached cautiously. He preceded him into the house and called Leah.

Leah emerged from the bath and spoke to José in Spanish. He responded in Spanish and followed her into the bathroom. Michael could hear Spanish between husband and wife.

It was unbelievable. A pregnant woman. All of them walking miles and miles from the leaky border, scattering from the fence, heading north, getting caught, sent back, coming again.

He thought of his own people coming from Europe a century ago, poor, overwhelmed.

Leah surfaced again from the bathroom conclave, primed to address him. "José and Lupe are worried about what you intend to do with them."

"I don't intend to do anything. What were they intending to do?"

"They were on their way to Los Angeles. They were told about places along this route through the mountains where they could find temporary shelter, sometimes food and water, sometimes a little work. It's a kind of underground railroad. I didn't know such a thing existed. I didn't know they took routes so far inland."

"But Lupe can't travel now, can she?"

"Obviously she can't do a lot of walking. And the baby is a problem. They can get rides on the highway, but it's dangerous."

"Do they have a place to go in Los Angeles?"

"If they do, they won't tell us."

"They can stay here for a while. What about the baby? Is it okay?"

"He seems to be healthy enough. A little scrawny. A few weeks early, according to Lupe. And Lupe seems to be all right."

"Shouldn't she see a doctor?"

"Even if they had money for a doctor, it would be risky. They would like a birth certificate for the baby, of course."

"A birth certificate?"

"The baby could claim citizenship."

"This whole thing is insane."

"You're just discovering the world's insanity? Anyway, if you want to help, they will need supplies, food. How long are you going to be here?"

"I have to return to Texas. I suppose we could stock the kitchen with food. Is it possible for someone to drive them to LA?"

"Immigration people are everywhere. They patrol, they set up road blocks. It would risky for anyone giving them a ride."

It was ironic, getting caught up in a conspiracy to defy the federal government. Mark had obviously participated in an arrangement, however loose, his shed known to the illegals. And there had been no hesitancy on his own part, or Leah's (and she an employee of the county welfare department) or Vanessa's to aid and abet.

"Perhaps, since you speak Spanish, you could stay with Lupe and José while Vanessa and I go in her car for supplies in Alpine. Your car is loaded with stereo gear anyway."

Leah hesitated, then nodded. Was she frightened of being alone with the Mexicans? The Mexicans seemed gentle and vulnerable. Under stress, Leah's eyes shifted from contact.

"You'll need to buy not only food, but baby supplies, diapers and baby oil and powder, and female supplies for Lupe." She spoke to the window.

"Baby bottles, milk?"

"Lupe is breast feeding, of course." She returned to the bathroom. The "of course" was another put down. Did she resent everybody?

Vanessa emerged. "Lupe should have a kimono or a dressing gown of some sort while she waits for her clothes to dry."

He went into Mark's bedroom. It seemed an intrusion to search through his clothes. There were not many. Not a single tie in sight. Everything was informal: jeans, shirts, sandals.

He found a plaid robe and remembered suddenly it was one Mark's mother had given him for Christmas after he returned from Iraq. Janice had sent him out to buy it for him. It appeared not to have been worn. He took it to Vanessa.

"Did Leah speak to you about shopping?" he said.

"Yes. I'll be happy to take you in a minute. Ill take the robe to Lupe, and when the washer stops, I'll put her clothes in the dryer."

"How is José taking all of this?"

"He looks grateful, but I don't think he is sure he can trust us."

9 VANESSA PARSONS

Michael Horne was a soft touch. The car was loaded with more food and supplies than Lupe and José could possibly use if they stayed only a week. Did Lupe know about disposable diapers and maxi-pads? Seeing her thin body, the sagging skin of her abdomen, the caked blood, had gotten to her. It made her more aware of the animal nature about herself she preferred not to think about. She glanced sideways at Michael.

"You all right?" she said over the rattles and wind whistling in.

"Tired. It's been a long day."

He had earned being tired. His son's funeral, the Mexican illegals with a bloody new-born baby on his son's property, strangers bothering him about computers and stereos. She felt a burst of sympathy for him that put down her customary cynicism at upper crust white types. She caught his reflection in the windshield: a bemused, russet face in the last colors of the sun going down.

The valley was growing dark. The sun was falling quickly behind the mountains. The muting shades of colors made it beautiful - if you liked desert scenes. She turned the car headlights on as they climbed through brush over the rutty road.

Lights were on in the house. José met them at the door, eyes wide at the quantity of things he helped carry in. Lupe appeared in her own freshly washed clothes, holding the baby, now swaddled deep in a bath towel, in such a way as to invite inspection. Michael touched the infant's curled fist with his finger.

Leah hovered, distant and dour. Was she biased against Hispanics as well as blacks? She had been helpful and efficient with Lupe and the baby. But under her overt busyness there had to be hidden cysts of anger.

They stored food in cabinets and in the refrigerator.

She hoped Lupe and José made it to LA and some kind of future.

She could tell them about LA: a forecast of the future of the world, an endless city with hundreds of nationalities clustered in hundreds of ghettoes where the lives of three Mexican innocents could come to nothing and mean zilch.

She returned to the living room and the computer. She knew there was nothing there that could help her. If the bastard had to shoot himself, why hadn't he just done it, instead of fucking up her life in the process? Why should he have given a shit about a graduate student, black, female, collecting and arranging the imaginary world inside a bag of novels for a dissertation that no one would ever read, except the committee that had to as part of their paid, professional duties?

She was sinking into a deep funk. She was the Mexican baby of the Lit department, and there was no neat, kind old biologist to provide food and protection on her way to a smoggy north of promises.

"I've got to get back," Leah said. "It's dark already."

She wore her official face. The Mexicans washed and dried, the provender purchased and put away, her case load for the day completed. She was looking at the wall.

"Would you please explain to José and Lupe that they are welcome to stay in the house for a week or two, however long it takes for Lupe to feel up to traveling?" Michael took out his wallet. "I don't have much cash left, but here is a hundred and forty dollars. Maybe it will help."

Leah hesitated. She turned to José and Lupe and translated. Michael handed the money to José. José accepted the money, his eyes betraying wonderment. Lupe's eyes filled with tears. She approached Michael, took his hand and kissed it. And made the sign of the cross.

Leah translated again: "Lupe says they are grateful to you and the Virgin of Guadalupe for your kindness to them."

"Wish them luck for me," Michael said, looking moved himself, and embarrassed. She was touched by his momentary awkwardness.

Leah translated, turned abruptly, then back. "Thank you for helping me," she said tightly. She strode out ungracefully.

When Leah had gone, Michael raised his eyes questioningly.

"I'm ready when you are," she said, smiling.

"Okay. But you didn't find anything in Mark's computer stuff, did you?"

"Nothing. I suppose it was unreasonable to think there might be something here."

"There's a filing cabinet in the garage. Let's take a peek anyway."

She followed as he groped and found the light. The old Volvo gave her an eerie feeling. She had seen Mark driving it on the campus. Michael thumbed the files, occasionally lifting one to look at it. With a file in hand, he stopped. She could read the file tab from an angle, It said "Michael Horne." Michael opened it, read for a moment, closed it, standing quiet. He brushed his sandy hair from his forehead and rubbed his eyes with the back of his free hand.

"You okay?" she said.

"I didn't know he had anything of mine."

She waited. It was none of her business. He kept the file and closed the cabinet. She was beginning to have the feeling that he was not only kind, but more complicated than she had realized. He drew himself straight.

"Do you know any Spanish?"

"Very little."

"Can you tell them that I might return to the house tomorrow. I don't want them to be frightened. I just want to look through Mark's files again."

"I'll give it a try."

When they returned to the living room they found José where

they had left him. Lupe was sitting on the sofa. The infant was making sounds.

"*Señor Horne,*" she said, pointing to Michael, "*aquí mañana. Comprende?*"

"*Sí. Comprendo*, José said.

"*Muy bien,*" she said.

"*Muy bien,* he said, smiling.

Michael shook José's hand. He went to Lupe and patted the baby gently. Vanessa followed, shaking José's hand, and smiling at Lupe.

Blessed by the Virgin of Somewhere, surely, they started down from the dark mountains to the lit-up city and endless housing developments. How strange it was to be caught up suddenly in the lives of people she didn't know. And in the death of someone she barely knew who had wronged her without reason.

10 *MICHAEL HORNE*

He sat in a chair near the window overlooking downtown San Diego. There had been a message from the crematorium saying his son's ashes were ready to be picked up. They had tried to sell him a fancy urn, but what was the point of an expensive temporary container, if Mark's ashes were to be scattered over the ocean? His hands ached and he kneaded them gently. He should take his prednisone. He was exhausted.

Flowers from his temporary colleagues at the Institute in Galveston were waiting for him. He felt separated from himself. The buildings in his view were part of a world other than his own. He was somewhere out of time.

Mark's file lay on the bed beside him. Vanessa, a sharp observer, had seen his shock when he found it. The will had said that the papers were to go to him. Mark had meant him to find the file. Letters from him to Mark from ages back, college years, two letters from Iraq. Were there clues in the letters about his reasons for suicide? And a xeroxed copy of the section of his diary about Noah's death. Mark had broken into his father's life to discover the manner of Noah's dying. What had the diary meant to him? He picked up his diary and read it again.

June 5, Evening
Beyond the colossal wall of the Sierra Nevada, an absolute schism:
Tuolumne Meadows, wet, green, with patches of snow - and the
sheer fall east from Tioga Pass into the desert almost ten thousand
feet down. The road clutches the side of the mountain, every distance
visible. I descend into a moonscape. The sun is eclipsed by the
Sierras behind me.

I sit in my pup tent outside Bishop in the last light, making these
notes, putting down, finally, the truth about Noah.

Janice suspects I come here to escape. She has always been unhappy
at my annual pilgrimages to the desert - not that she has any desire
to accompany me to this "god-forsaken" place; it's that I'm doing
something she has never been able to understand.

The first time Noah and I came to this country of gravel, boulders,
scrawny desiccated plants, it had the character of a skeleton. The
desert is sky. It does not come to you in small blocks from between
buildings or leak through the branches of trees; it comes from
everywhere at once. At sunrise and sunset the long rolling valleys
are suffused with color - reds, pinks, lavenders, purples, grays - as
the mountains ascend into light or deepen in shadow. The day
between is sun-white.

Too dark to write now. I will get into my sleeping bag and try to
sleep. In the smell of sage, to the whine of coyotes.

June 6, Midmorning
I am resting in a dry creek bed, in the shadows of a clump of bushes,
off the trail because of a motorcycle gang that roared by half and
hour ago. I heard them in the distance and took cover. I am outraged
that their kind come here to tear up the surface of the ground and
pollute the air. Their marks will stay. Everything does because of
the arid climate. The evidence of their passing will remain like
Indian paintings for centuries, signs of our civilization.

Coming to Terms

I sit in the growing heat, sipping water from my canteen, eating a dry sandwich. Is my thinking, too, subject to evolutionary coercion?

Why does a good man die? As a biologist, I m obliged to find my question irrelevant. There is no good or evil in nature - only strategies for survival.

We are on our evolutionary ride. We do our propagation dances, protect our turf, eat our way through our lives, and die. An "unnatural" growth of human cells? Viruses? Catastrophes? Here the truth is clear: everything is nature.

June 6, Noon
I pause to sip some water and rest. I am climbing to a higher elevation beyond West Guard Pass and Cedar Flats, north toward the area of the Bristlecone Pine, the oldest living plant on earth. It's slow going. I'm getting older, too, puppet to my helical strings.

Noah and I came here every year after graduate school all those years. Then one last time together. He hated to see evidence of more and more off-the-road four wheel drive vehicles penetrating even the most remote parts of the high desert. Noah was wont to wax a bit mystical about ecology. Ecology for him was a kind of religion which holds that nature has a balance that cannot be disturbed without eternal damage. Though we came to the desert ourselves, I think he sometimes felt humans should be deleted from the earth to preserve its natural state. But isn't man a part of nature? Is there something different about human conduct, as opposed to that of other animals, that is at odds with nature?

Other primates have modes of conduct, and they scold their fellows when they misbehave, but these are social codes. Man is the only creature capable of conscious evil toward his habitat. But "evil" in any context is a human concept.

Noah yearned to have sense of being part of nature, and that's why we returned the last time. We drove as far as we could, until the car was stalling in the high altitude and on the loose surface of the

41

trail. Then we walked, as I am walking now, retracing our steps. We had to rest very few minutes because of his weakness. We brought a bottle of wine (he couldn't eat; they had been feeding him intravenously), a blanket, a shovel.

June 6, Mid-afternoon
I have arrived sooner than I anticipated, out of breath because of the altitude and the physical effort. The site is unchanged: rocks at the four corners of the grave, and loosely over the middle of the length. We dragged them here before digging to make sure we could find enough. Noah tried to carry some, but he was too weak. He became faint and sat shaking while I completed the rock hauling and the digging - through gravel hard as concrete, and a network of resisting roots.

We waited while Noah gasped and tried to recover some strength.

His great wish was to do it the way he had planned it. He had managed to do everything else, mustering enough strength to unhook the tubes, leave his hospital bed, put on the clothes I had left for him, and descended in the service elevator to the service entrance where I waited in my station wagon. He crawled into the back and onto an air mattress. I covered him with a light blanket and we started our long trip from Berkeley to Bishop, Big Pine, and Cedar Flats.

He had been fearful he couldn't make it, that someone would spot him and try to stop us. Without the stuff going into his veins, he grew weaker and the pain came back. He could barely walk when we left the car. He spirits perked up when he saw that we had actually reached his beloved terrain, but the flesh was frail.

As I sit here now recovering my breath, I wonder we made it at all, let alone accomplished the rest. As I promised, I have returned each year since to make sure he is undisturbed. There is no one else. Noah never married and seemed not to have any family - though he had many friends at the university and played godfather to Mark.

Coming to Terms

Distance can heal, yet there are moments when the heart erupts with all its hoarded pain. The event in its moment is all shock. Memory makes the connections and masses them in the face of one's powerlessness.

The first year I returned alone, I wondered, irrationally, whether Noah knew I was there. He wanted his consciousness to go on. But consciousness is simply another mutation that has happened in our push to survive as a species, like a paw, or a brightly colored feather. When the synapses stop firing, it's silence.

Noah believed, or wanted to believe, that there was some mysterious connection between plants, animals, humans, our entire past as each cell replaced itself, and that, perhaps, if we listened carefully enough, we could sense, however dimly, our whole chain of being back to the sea. When he first confided his speculations, as he called them, I laughed. He was too good a biologist to argue his absurdities; nevertheless, he thought about them when we came to the desert.

When he felt well enough, or said he did, I opened the bottle of wine. I had to hold the mouth of the bottle to his lips while he tried to drink. His throat was almost completely blocked by then.

"Pour some on the ground," he said in a thin voice.

"A libation?" I said.

He tried to smile. Tears were running down his misshapen face.

"I'm sorry," he said. "I don't want to be weak, but I can't help it." After a while, he said: "It's time." I nodded, not trusting my voice.

I climbed into the hole and helped him down. I wrapped him in the blanket, and he lay in the dirt. I took the gun from my jacket and placed it in his hands. Hands shaking, he pointed it toward his head. After a moment, his hands dropped. "I'm too weak," he said. His head fell to one side and he drew it back with great effort. "You'll have to help me," he said. "I can't," I said.

He tried again to lift the gun, and this time he could not hold it high enough. "Please," he said. I held the gun for him and placed his finger on the trigger. His finger twitched but did not move the trigger. I put my finger on his and pushed. The trigger lever was stiff and I had to push hard, the frail flesh of his finger crushed beneath my own. The gun fired with a heavy jolt.

I covered his blasted face with the blanket, climbed out and filled the hole with dirt. It was dusk when I began and nearly dark when I finished placing the stones. I cut a small branch with some difficulty and ran it over the ground to disguise the digging and our tracks. The stones still mark the site, as they have all these years, their arrangement looking almost natural.

June 6, Dusk
Maggots, I suppose, have long since eaten his body away, the distortions of cells, the ugly suppurations. A skeleton now, like the desert itself, clean, dry, he rests in the gravel - itself loose remnants of something else, other shapes now gone.

My work with genes seems remote at these times. After all we learn, after all we are, all everything is, everything comes to nothing. Noah's death taught me the randomness of our living. He longed deeply to believe there was some purpose to it all. But look at the universe. We invent meaning and beg the question as to purpose.

I survive, go on learning, and, without purpose, come to this site as though I were performing an ancient ceremony. Here in the nakedness of nature, a reverence of sorts.

Mark had underlined a sentence in the excerpt: "Yet there are moments when the heart erupts with all its hoarded pain."

There were so many losses in a life, and the irremediable pain lingered like the scars of one's physical history. His sense of time when he worked in his lab, or thought about his work, was nearly seamless. But individual human events seemed to occur haphazardly, in crowds of other events, messy with the miscellany of things that preceded or strayed to the side.

Coming to Terms

William Faulkner's attempts to bring all the pertinent history to bear upon a single event, and to capture it in a single sentence that sometimes ran on for pages, had exhilarated him with the notion that one could understand what was happening at a particular moment - if one could set it in its historical perspective.

But that was fiction. The construction of history was itself an exercise in selectivity and invention. And history was full of dead ends. Perhaps Heisenberg's principle of indeterminacy could be made to apply: you couldn't simultaneously comprehend for certain both where you were and the flow of history in time.

The affairs and feelings that defined the torments of Mark's life - anguish at his mother's death; the corrosion of ideals; hurt and anger at anger and violence; religious and political terrorism; deceitful government; corrupt politicians, those who sent young men to die in deserts half-way around the world - were intelligible enough. But others had not reacted in his way. These were not uncommon traits, nor did they represent rare conduct the history of the human tribe. There was something in Mark's original character that caused him to suffer differently and beyond his endurance.

11 *LEAH STEIN*

She poured orange juice into a screwdriver glass, added a slug of vodka, stirred it with her finger, and carried it to her room to dress. Orin was in the master suite shower. She could hear the water go on and she turned her own off in the guest suite.

She was putting on her eyelashes when the phone rang. She started toward the kitchen to answer but it stopped. Orin had answered in the master bedroom. She heard bare feet padding through the kitchen, a knock on the door. She was in her slip.

"Leah?"

She opened the door to find Orin in his slacks and hairy bare chest. Her heart thumped.

"It's Lydia's friends at the hospital. They say we'd better come right away."

Orin had arrived only yesterday, after her call telling him the end was near. Lydia hadn't wanted him to come at all. She didn't want him to see how she looked, wasted away to nothing in a year. Lydia's appearance had shocked him out of his laid-back urbanity. She had once been beautiful.

When she saw Lydia's friends who took turns visiting her were all there, she knew it had happened. Tears were running down their cheeks. Lydia had been so dear a friend to all of them, and to her

46

during the year she had lived with her.

"We didn't want to summon the nurse until you got here," Mary said to Orin. "We didn't want them to take her away."

Orin kissed Lydia's forehead. She went to stand by him as they gazed down at Lydia's shrunken, hairless skull. Orin walked to the corner of the room and leaned his head against the wall.

The nurse came in and asked them to leave. They straggled to the solarium at the end of the hall.

Leah embraced him, and he patted her on the back. She could hear his breath catching. He released himself from her grasp and went to the window. Birds flew up from the ledge beyond the glass as he approached.

Lydia's doctor appeared and motioned for Orin to follow him down the hall. The doctor placed his arm around Orin's shoulder and they talked. Beyond them, orderlies were trundling a body covered with a sheet toward the elevator. A sheet over Lydia's face. A body bag for Mark.

Orin returned to the solarium. "I gave permission for an autopsy." He wiped his eyes with his lapel handkerchief. "Thank you," he said to all of them. "We might as well go home. There is nothing more we can do here."

Her heart jumped when he spoke. But he didn't mean it that way. It was her temporary home while Lydia was alive. Orin's property entirely now. Orin embraced the women one after another.

When they reached the house, Orin headed for the master suite. She went to the kitchen. The house was empty without Lydia. And her friends. What would Orin do with the house? Living in Chicago, he didn't need it. In the incredibly inflated San Diego market it would be worth a lot of money.

She dropped a slice of bread in the toaster and poured herself some orange juice and added a jolt of vodka. At some point Orin would want food.

The telephone calls began and people started coming by. She resented their intrusion. Orin emerged from the master suite to accept their condolences. Lydia would have been pissed off, but he really did act shaken. There were arrangements to be made, undertakers to be dealt with, and he seemed unaware. She would help him. Lydia hadn't said so, but she was sure she would have chosen to be cremated. She would tell Orin. She had had her father cremated. She had made the decision for Mark, and Dr. Horne had not contradicted her.

People finally stopped coming. Orin sipped a scotch. She went to his side and looked at the ocean. She touched his hand; he patted her on the arm. She wanted to hold him. They had both loved Lydia. Orin stepped back from the windows and went back to the master suite again, quietly closing the door behind him. She picked up the empty cups and glasses and carried them to the kitchen. The dishwasher was full. She added soap and started it going. The noise made her sleepy. She bit into a slice of cold toast, stirred herself another screwdriver, and lay on the sofa in the family room.

Orin was shaking her. The house was dark except for the light coming from the kitchen. She had been dreaming about her father going away. She was calling out to him, but he kept on going.

"I made an omelet," Orin said.

He returned to the kitchen and set up the eating bar. He still had the tan that belonged in La Jolla. She followed him into the kitchen.

He slid a spatula under the omelet, broke it in half, and laid each half deftly on a plate.

"Voila!" he said.

She was watching a late night rerun. She had to force herself to eat. Lydia dying. Her father dying with that look on his face. Mark with a hole in his temple. She could almost see Orin as a corpse. He was a son of a bitch like her father.

Was it too soon to ask him whether he would sell the house to her? If she didn't ask, he would turn it over to an agent. If she bought the house, would Orin come back to visit her?

"You're not eating very much," Orin said.

"You sound like my Jewish mother."

Orin laughed. It was the first time she had heard him laugh since he arrived. He used to laugh all the time, the jolly bastard. He refilled his glass of wine, held up the bottle and lifted his eyebrows.

"I'll stay with this," she said. She raised her empty vodka glass.

He took it, poured in a generous shot of vodka, added ice, and handed it back to her with another one of his grand flourishes. How could Lydia have been taken in by this ersatz Clark Gable?

Orin rinsed off the plates at the sink. He saw that the dishwasher was full of clean dishes and began putting them away in the shelf above the eating bar.

She started to rise and found herself swaying. She sat down. The room was spinning. Orin leaned over her.

"You okay?" he said.

"I'm all right."

"Sure?" He was there, his face close. Did he really care? He was being polite.

"I'm fine," she said. She was not fine.

"Okay. I'm beat and I'm going to bed," he said.

"Like to be tucked in?" Someone else said it, a little girl in her voice.

His face took on an odd look. "'Night," he said. He patted her on the shoulder, the way he had patted the death watch on their shoulders in the morning. A touch that was gesture of sympathy and dismissal at once. She should want only what she could expect.

The house was empty again. Empty without Orin. Empty without Lydia and Lydia's friends. If she bought the house, would they be her friends? She got up slowly and walked into the living room. Her walk was unsteady. She could barely see the ocean. The sun had sunk beneath a hedge of clouds and smog drifting south from Los Angeles. Was Orin staring out at the same gray ocean from the master bedroom? She heard water running in the shower. She could imagine his body, the lean contours, the dark skin, the hair on his chest she had seen in the morning. The sound of the shower stopped. It was quiet.

She went to the guest suite in a kind of daze. She removed her clothes and put on her peignoir. She felt shaky and shivery. She finished her drink and walked barefoot to the living room. She listened at the door of the master suite. The knob turned easily. The bedroom was dark save for a faint glow from the undraped windows.

"Orin?"

He started. He must have fallen asleep at once.

"Leah?"

She lay beside him and curved her arm over his chest.

"What are you doing?"

"I loved her so much." She kissed him on the ear.

He put hands on her shoulders and pushed her away. "I know. But you had better go back to your room."

"I want to sleep with you." The voice again that sounded like her voice when she was a little girl.

"You've had too much vodka, Leah. I'll take you back to your own bed."

He lifted her, one arm under her bent knees, the other under her shoulders as though she weighed nothing at all. She was helpless. He was so strong. The peignoir fell from her breasts. He carried her to her room through the semi-darkness of the house. He'd closed her peignoir and covered her with the sheet to her chin as though she were a child.

Tears were puddling her mascara. He was gone.

She kicked the sheet off and wrapped her arms about herself, sobbing, rocking the bed. She didn't want the house anymore. She didn't want anything anymore. She had wanted to comfort him. She wanted to fill the void left by Lydia. Was Lydia there? Was her father there? Bloody-headed Mark? There was no one there. She had no one.

12 *TOM NEWTON*

He had just gotten in the door when he heard the phone ringing. By the time he reached the extension, it had stopped. The caller had stopped before the fifth ring that triggered the answering machine. He should get a cellular like everybody else, but he hated being tied to one. If it was important, the caller would ring again. He left his tennis racket by the phone and went upstairs to his shower.

He had let Harry win the last game, and Harry knew he had, and Harry knew he knew. Harry had retired three years ago as an editor, but he still wrote reviews for *The Times*. His father used to say he did more business on the golf course than he did in his office, and given the amount he had made, and passed on to his son, it had clearly been a successful formula. Besides, his father liked to play golf. He was not sure tennis courts were the same, but it helped to be friendly with Harry when Harry reviewed the books he published. And besides, he liked to play tennis.

Given that his new venture into publishing had not yet done all that well in the three years he had been in it, it was a good thing his father had left him what he left him. He had lost less last year and calculated he might show a profit this year, if the novel about the Texas country western singer and his tempestuous love affair with the wife of an oil baron who was in deep trouble with the IRS continued to sell the way it had started. He had barely been able to skim through it, but he had given in to his new senior editor. That tough old cookie talked to him aft as though she were the skipper of the firm, but she had had more than a dozen best sellers to her credit at other houses, as well as successful secondary rights sales, so he needed her. You had to publish bad books that sold if you were going to be able to publish good ones that didn't. And you had to tolerate old bitches when they were as good as Harriet. Had he sold out?

He reached blindly for a towel and found it where Wendy always left it when she did the upstairs. The phone rang again and this time, still wet, he caught it.

"Tom?"

It was Laurie, as he figured it might be.

"Yo."

"I'm in the city. I'm too tired to come out to Connecticut. I'll stay here tonight and come out tomorrow. You all right?"

"Fine. How are you?"

"Beat. Otherwise, okay."

"How did it go?"

"All right, I guess. A little weird. I'll tell you about it tomorrow. Love."

"Love."

He hung up. Beat she might be, after the funeral and the flight from San Diego, but she'd bed down with her jock tonight. Well, okay. He'd bed down with Orina. She had let him know at the Club, looking sexy in her tennis skirt, that Phil was in London. That little smile and the twinkle in her eye. He hated to think of Laurie and her jock. He loved Laurie, and if he was going to keep her, he had to tolerate her affairs. Shit. He dialed Orina's house.

She answered the phone on the first ring. She must have been sitting on it.

"How about two bachelors having dinner?"

"Your place or mine?"

He laughed. Not one for small talk, that one.

"Here. I've got a saddle of salmon in the freezer."

"What time?"

"Eightish?"

"I'll be there."

Jesus. His dong was beginning to swell already. When he hung up, his eye caught the manuscript of a collection of poems on his bedside table. Jill, one of his young fiction editors, had a boy friend who was a poet. He had won some prizes but he ought to have a book, she said, and she thought the firm ought to do some poetry. How much money did she want the firm to lose? Prestige, she said. College bookstores carry poetry, and even Barnes and Noble. Christ. Prestige or profit, was that the choice? There were no real bookstores anymore, just big chains. You had to get reviews and you couldn't get a book reviewed unless the author were already a celebrity. You had to buy hype. The bloody corporate publishers were in cahoots with the bloody big chains. Books were produced and marketed as though they were chickens. Buy them by the thousands, discount them, sell them fast, and dump the ones that don't sell by morning. Publishing and selling books were businesses, but books were something else, weren't they? Was he being stupid?

And now internet sales. Maybe that was a way to get around chain and media control. Were "instant books" going to change publishing? You wouldn't have to keep a taxable inventory. Maybe he should sell his press. But what about books, print, the feel in your hand?

René Foutre was the guy's name. Was that a name? He thought that was a dirty word in French. From Louisiana, hot out of the bayou. He opened the manuscript box and started a poem at random:

LETTER TO HUGO

Air is swamp. Where ground is high, a bait
shop or a bar, shacks on stilts
like spindly birds. Rusty shrimpers wobble
on the dirty tide. Rheumatic oaks cling
like washed-out whores to their familiar streets...

That was poetry? Where was the beauty in it? Did Wordsworth ever write about things as ugly as this? And who was Hugo? He dropped the manuscript back in its box and picked up another.

Deciding to Die, its title announced. By a self-styled ethicist at The University of Texas Medical Branch in Galveston.

Wasn't that where Laurie's father had gone on a sabbatical to do something on scientific ethics? Laurie had suggested he might want to look at what her father wrote. Wasn't that more appropriate for a subsidized university press? In the public eye scientists were either gods or Frankensteins. Maybe the big God was both. Besides, he didn't like to think about dying.

Michael Horne was a nice guy. Except, Jimmy had remarked, to other scientists who didn't agree with him. Bright, a Midwesterner who married into West Coast money and flourished at Berkeley as an academic. Laurie said he had once been nominated for a Nobel.

Mark's suicide had to have hit him hard. He had met Mark once. Prickly bastard. Laurie didn't even suggest he go to the funeral. She knew how he felt about death. When his shrink heard that he didn't want to think about dying, he asked why he thought he didn't want to. Silly question. Who in his right mind would want to? Right now he was going to think about baking a saddle of salmon, chilling some Chenin Blanc, making a salad. And Orina.

13 *LAURIE NEWTON*

She kept drifting off. It was not only that she was tired, but that after sex she always felt sleepy. Her friends claimed it was supposed to be the other way around; males went to sleep and females wanted to talk. She got sleepy and Billy wanted to talk. Mostly about himself. Usually about sports. About the most important days of his life when he was a football player at Wake Forest. Beefy in both body and mind, he was overpowering in bed, and, though she wasn't masochistic, she liked being overpowered. And then she wanted Billy to go away and let her sleep.

And now he was smoking and talking again. She had intended to break off her affair with Billy. He wasn't worth his chitchat. But what would she do for entertainment then? The last time she went to confession, Father Feeney had given her hell. What did Father Feeney know about women's needs? She felt bad about doing this to Tom. Tom loved her. Not that he was all that faithful himself. Last summer she had discovered that Tom had screwed Orina in the swimming pool. Maybe he had been a little casual on other occasions, too. Tom was something of a bore, but he was basically a good guy. It was just that her life was full of the same things over and over. Nothing really important ever happened to her. She didn't know what something important would be, but it surely wasn't anything that had happened yet.

The most important thing in Billy's life was behind him. At least it had happened and he could talk about it. Now he was a broker, churning over his clients' stocks.

She had her religion. It was her mother's religion. Her father had agreed to be married in church, but that was the extent of his participation. He didn't try to dissuade anyone in the family from belief, even though it contradicted science. He was impatient with creationists; otherwise it was laissez faire. He was more moral than anyone else she knew. Believe what you need to believe, but don't go for any hocus pocus, he told her when she went to a convent school.

Her mother had spent her days in a fantasy world of religious lore, but she had performed her conventional duties: she had had her children christened and instructed and took them to mass. It was like their piano lessons, something they learned to do, but not well.

Jimmy had married in the church. Even so, he had gotten a divorce. She was religious out of uncertainty. Mark had been opposed to religion from the beginning. He blamed religion for the evils of the world. More people had been tortured and murdered in the name of religion than for any other cause in human history, he shouted in that awful harangue he had subjected them to when she and Tom had visited him in San Diego on one of Tom's manuscript buying trips. Tom, not exactly devout, had been shocked. That guy is a madman, he said afterward. She defended Mark. She hadn't told Tom that Mark had been the only one she could go to as a teenager needing an abortion, and that he taken her to a doctor and stayed with her and was gentle and kind about the whole thing. She hadn't told Father Feeney either. It had happened such a long time ago. It was there always like the mole on her right breast, hidden, except when she looked in the mirror.

She slept at last and when she woke Billy was gone. Daylight was leaching through the curtains. She had been dreaming about Mark's coffin gliding from their view into the furnace. In her dream Mark was still alive. Her mother was there, too, trying to tell Father something was wrong. They were waiting for Father to straighten it all out before it was too late. No one could do anything, and the coffin was moving.

She felt disoriented again, the way she had at the funeral, the way she had in Berkeley when her mother told her about dying and bodies waiting for the resurrection.

She struggled to the bath.

14 *MICHAEL HORNE*

He had purchased extra carrying cases, a special one to bring back the Miró prints, another to carry the potpourri of papers he had discovered in the filing cabinet, and a small one for the box of Mark's ashes. He hesitated to look at the papers, even after going all the way to Alpine again to secure them.

José and Lupe did not seem at ease in the house. They appeared to be fearful of disturbing even the slightest stick of furniture. He tried to tell José that they should make themselves at home, save that that was beyond his Spanish and José's English. They smiled at each other. He patted the baby. He gathered the files. The house ought to belong to the Mexicans, he thought. Since they were illegals it was not possible. And José needed to find work. What could he find in Alpine?

It was an odd assortment, including transcripts of Mark's studies at UCLA. The grades were all A's, except for one grade of B in physics. Mark had never revealed how he fared, though he informed them when he got his degree. That secretive trait had been part of his character since elementary school. If he hadn't had to have his report cards signed by a parent, they would never had seen them. He had done well except in "listening" and "social attitudes" where he received U's. The U's had elected conferences with teachers.

Janice, anxious in private, aloof in conference, was gentle with Mark who accepted her consolations while ignoring any blandishments for improvement. As a father, he had failed to see the signs he should have seen. It was only later that realized that being bright and independent and being bright and in trouble were not the same. Had they recognized Mark's problems then, would it have made a difference?

Mark and his mother seemed to have a special relationship, tacit, undefined. Janice was inclined to be vague about some things, and he had accepted their bond as natural, a spiritual connection of the sort she was wont to lay claim to.

And Mark and Noah had gotten along well. Noah had a way with kids. He would take them into his confidence and activities as though what he proposed was what they really wanted to do. He took Mark camping with in the Sierras to take in the "systems of nature." They collected botanical specimens and Mark had a collection of his own.

But Mark's eleventh Christmas had turned into a nightmare of hurt and embarrassment. Noah had given Mark a microscope. It was a good one and Mark was clearly delighted with it. Janice reproved Noah for spending the amount of money he had for it.

"I got a good deal on it," Noah said. "Besides, since I don't have my own family to spend my money on, I can spend it as I please."

Noah smiled as he said it, but there was a wistful undertone. He didn't often refer to his personal life. He quickly began explaining to Mark how to use the microscope.

"Can I look at my specimens?"

"You can. I brought you some sample slides of other things, too." Noah reached into his pocket and pulled out a small case of slides. "When you've looked at these, we'll go find some live insects from the soil in your yard. I'll show you how to make slides."

They busied themselves with the microscope, and Jimmy, who had watched the proceedings with great interest, began to develop a forlorn face.

Noah, always sensitive, caught his look, and suggested Jimmy come out to the porch with him. Jimmy followed dubiously. Then came a yell of surprise, and Jimmy entered running to announce that Noah had given a two-wheeler dirt bike, and he wanted to ride it right away.

Janice told him he could if he stayed on the sidewalk. He accepted her condition and took off at a run.

"Does he know how to ride a two-wheeler?" he said.

"He's been riding other kids' bikes when they let him," Janice said.

"We collaborated," Noah said. "I get my inside information from Janice."

Janice brought out a doll Noah had bought for Laurie that was nearly as big as she. Laurie kissed Noah and hugged the doll tight and hummed to it. They laughed. But the day ended in disaster.

They had set their usual Christmas dinner for the late afternoon. Janice and Frieda, their housekeeper, cook, factotum and woman of all trades, had prepared turkey, ham, candied yams, pies, strudel (Frieda's specialty). The table had been laid out with decorations of flowers and pine boughs. The boys, frequently allowed to eat separately, were required on this occasion to eat with their elders. Jimmy bolted his food and obviously itched to leave for more bike riding. Mark remained silent. As she tended to Laurie's eating, and Laurie pretended to feed the doll, Janice spoke of a nephew graduating from Occidental and going into real estate with his father, her older brother.

"It's a good thing were not required to follow our fathers' occupations like the Hindus," Noah said, his pale face crinkling in amusement. "Since my father was a bartender in Elko, Nevada." They laughed. There was more to it, Michael knew. Noah's father had been jailed for running a prostitution operation.

"How did you ever get to Berkeley?" Janice said. She was always impressed by self-made people and had a knack for drawing them out. Along with her siblings, she was accustomed to her inherited money. A career was beyond her compass.

"On my thumb," Noah said. "I had graduated from high school by hook and by crook, but there was nothing to do in Elko that I had any interest in doing. I just took off for the big city. Which, for an inhabitant of Nevada in my day, was Reno. I worked for a while in a casino, first as a bus boy, then as a waiter. I took some courses at the university. I had always been keen about science, but my studies required more time than my work would allow. So I headed for California."

"And you found a job?"

"Same kind of job, as a waiter in Berkeley. It wasn't what I wanted to do. I got my records from Elko and a transcript from the University of Nevada at Reno, marched to the admissions office in Berkeley and asked to be admitted. Those were less crowded days at the university; but, even so, I think the woman in the admissions office must have been amused at this gangly kid from Elko, Nevada just popping in like that. My records were good, but not all that impressive. And I was out-of-state. I was admitted, but they weren't about to offer me a scholarship. I still had to go to work to pay my tuition, board and room."

"Can I go ride my bike? I'm all finished." Jimmy got his request in while Noah paused to drink some coffee.

Janice frowned, but granted him leave.

She said to Noah: "Where did you two meet?"

"In the biology lab. Where else?"

Michael laughed. "There weren't enough microscopes to go around that semester, so we had to share. We fought over who was going to use, and when, the microscope assigned to the two of us. That's how we met and became good friends."

"I'm glad you did," Janice said. "Otherwise Mark would not have gotten a microscope for Christmas."

"Even if you're not a Hindu," Noah said to Mark. "You can follow your father's footsteps and become a biologist. You can get a head start with the microscope."

"I don't want to follow in my father's footsteps."

There was a moment of silence. "You don't have to, dear," Janice said. "You can be anything you want to be."

"You should know that your father's making a name for himself in evolutionary biology," Noah said. "He's becoming a star in his field."

"I don't want to be like my father, a star, or anything else." His face was taut and white.

Noah was clearly taken aback. This was a side to Mark he had not seen before.

"You can leave the table now, Mark." Janice said. Her face

betrayed her effort to suppress her distress.

Michael swallowed his hurt and said nothing. Mark had never stated his resentment so openly before.

Mark got up and went into the living room. A moment later they heard a crash and glass breaking. They rose hurriedly and entered the living room to find the microscope sideways on the floor, slides scattered over the wood floor in the hallway. Mark had disappeared up the stairs; they could hear the sound of running steps. Janice foundered in tears. Laurie began to cry and Janice picked her up. Noah began to collect the slides. He straightened the microscope and arranged it properly on the table where it had been placed originally. He had tears in his eyes when he faced them.

"I'm sorry," he said. "What I said must have provoked him."

"He's never done a thing like that before," Janice said.

"It's okay, Michael said. "You couldn't have known he'd react to your suggestion like that. Kids go through these things."

But Mark had not gone through them. Janice had gone upstairs toting Laurie who was still crying and clutching her doll. Noah had left shortly after, patently mystified and embarrassed. Janice reported later that Mark cried when she tried to talk to him. Finally, in his mother's arms, he said he was sorry. Sorry for a scene that distressed his mother and hurt Noah? Sorry for what he had said and how he felt toward his father? Sophocles should have turned the irony of Oedipus's ignorance around. The father didn't know his own son.

He knew from his feeling toward his own father that the relationship could be difficult. Yet he had not hated his father. His father's death had taught him that. It was simply that he wanted to be free to be himself. Was that what Mark wanted?

That devastated Christmas would stay with him until he died. It would stay like other scars in his memory: fleeing south from the hordes of Chinese, the dead frozen where they fell. The forgotten war. Were Korea and Iraq the same? When a war had no clean ending, you lost belief. For years he had awakened from dreams in a sweat, hearing the clump of unseen artillery reaching closer, seeing the gaping mouths and eyes of the dead around him: American, Korean, Chinese. Now Iraq, another war. Politicians sending the young to die. And the grossly misnamed Patriot Act. Would freedom be lost because no one was safe?

Everything died and everything went on. Nature was at war, from lowly cells to their highest aggregations in human beings. He remembered his Lit class. They had debated Camus: we had the ability to choose to die, and that was the source of our freedom. Freedom? We were made up of genes that set us into what were; eternal chains of causes and effects bore upon us. Our environments impinged. We were carriers of DNA whose ultimate purpose was to create more DNA. Consciousness brought with it the illusion of choice. We were never safe. That, too, was an illusion.

Mark had gathered his psyche from his genes and his earliest years. He had to be what he was. He chose, in the illusion of his consciousness, to break his connection with the chain, a dead end among the billions of dead ends, his human body changed into gases and chemicals to be thrown into the sea.

Janice would say that Mark's consciousness was an aura. But there were no "auras". Self was a construct of consciousness; consciousness was a construct of the brain. Without the brain there was no consciousness, no self. There was nothing beyond. There was no lie in his culture he could accept that would assuage his loss.

15 *VANESSA PARSONS*

L-shaped houses of cracked, dirty stucco, cheek by jowl on streets lined with old rusty pick-up trucks and beat-up vans: this was home. It was a place where her dilapidated Mustang belonged. She hated it with all her soul. She would have made a U-turn and driven away, had it not been for her family. She breathed the acid smog of cars from the freeway that had no exit.

How could Kitty have let it happen? Mother had never secretive about the facts of life. Not after her husband left her with six kids and nothing to feed them with or pay the rent, who showed up with the empty gift of his put-on, suave presence when he was between gigs, or shady operations, or preaching stints.

Momma had told her everything when she was ten. "I isn't doin nothin," Vanessa had said. "I know," her mother said. "I'm telling you now *afore* you do something. First thing *don't* do it. When the time comes, use protection. And it's really stupid to get pregnant out of wedlock and get stuck with a lot of kids. And don't forget the guy who sleeps with you has already slept with Lord knows how many other girls and he carries all the diseases they got." Momma had learned the hard way, brought up by a religious mother who thought merely mentioning the word sex was a sin. She must have told Kitty all that. What went wrong?

Kitty was number five. Momma used to count them. Vanessa, then Joel, then Jeb, then Benny, then Kitty, then Lila. Kitty must be fifteen. Not out of high school yet. Shit. Kitty was the prettiest, and mature at fifteen. A prime target for some big dude on the street.

Her mother tried to keep a sharp eye on all of them, but she had to work. It had fallen to Vanessa, once she was old enough, to take care of the younger ones. Grandma Marybelle had taken care of them until her sister Hootie got ill and she had to go back to Alabama to take care of her. Then there was no one to help.

Joel was in the army and Jeb was going to the community college and Benny was a drop-out and without a job and not wanting to go to back to school. Momma pushed education on all of them. Kitty in high school, and now what? Lila had just started.

Lila was perky, Momma said. Maybe she would make it.
She was sitting in her car when Benny's funny face appeared upside down in her windshield. He had crawled on top of he car without her knowing it. He made more funny faces. His face was as flexible as rubber. She couldn't help but laugh.

He slid off the roof when she got out of her car. "Hey," he said.

He was embarrassed when she hugged him. "How have you been?"

"Okay, I guess. What you here for?"

"Can't I come home to see you all?"

"You don't come home all that much. Must be some special reason."

"I'm teaching freshman English and I'm trying to write a book I have to write for my degree. I come home when I can."

They walked to the house together. Benny stopped at the door. "I ain't goin in. Momma's mad at me."

"What for?"

"Don't know. She just mad."

Her mother appeared at the door and opened her arms. "You look skinny."

"You always say that. I'm not skinny. You look skinny."

"I been skinny all my life, 'cept when I carried you kids."

Her mother did look skinny. She didn't eat much at anytime, no matter what she cooked. She had cooked for a white family in

65

San Marino for a long time until they moved away. Then for a small restaurant in Pasadena. Now she cooked for two-bit cafe in Eagle Rock, riding the bus to and from for hours. She seemed older than her age, but neat, as always.

"Is Kitty here?"

Her mother looked toward the door to make sure Benny wasn't listening in. "I sent her to the store. I was hoping to talk to you first, anyway."

"How did it happen?"

"Same way it always happens."

"Who's the guy?"

"A drop-out that hangs out at the car wash next to the school. He dries and polishes. Minimum wage. Minimum intelligence. Minimum chance of ever doing anything." She shook her head.

"She in love with him?"

"She loves the attention. He's tall and handsome. Talks smooth like your father. She's in love with being made love to by a big, handsome guy. What else is new in this world?"

"How long has it been?"

"At least six weeks." Her mother sat in her favorite chair. There was a Bible on the little table beside the chair. She didn't read it all that much, unlike Grandma Marybelle who read it all the time. Her mother read books from the public library, anything and everything. She had copied her mother.

"What does she want to do about it?"

"She wants to keep it, like I said on the phone. She thinks if she has his baby, this guy will really love her. Course he'll just take off and dry cars somewheres else. And take up with another dumb piece of tail."

"Kitty isn't a dumb piece of tail."

"Way she acts. Way you act is the way you are. I brought her up the way I brought you up. Least she could take precautions. I think, if you want to know, she did it on purpose 'cause she thought she could trap him. That's what I think. Is that a dumb piece of tail?"

"I can't believe it."

"Ask her."

Her mother rested her hand on the Bible without noticing it. It was a familiar place to put her hand. The house looked the same. Plants she had had to water. Old furniture covered with rugs her grandmother knitted. The same light fixture in the ceiling that didn't work. The painting of a storm at sea her father had brought home from God knows where. She wanted to get her mother out of here. She wanted to help her brothers and sisters. She had dreamed of doing all that for a long time. She had to make it.

"Have you heard from Joel lately?"

"He's being assigned to Iraq."

She caught her breath. Little Joel.

Her mother was on the verge of tears.

"And Jeb?"

"He doin all right. He works hard."

"Benny?"

"He find hisself one of these days." Momma liked Benny. He made her laugh. When she wasn't mad at him for misbehaving.

High heels clicked on the front walk and Kitty backed the front door open, carrying two bags of groceries, turned and saw Vanessa.

"Hey, Vanessa, what you doin here?" She glanced at her mother, guessing. Momma was wearing her usual enigmatic face.

"Hey, Kitty."

"Lemme put these groceries in the kitchen."

"I'll help you." She followed her sister. Kitty put the bags on the counter, and they hugged.

"Get your Ph.D. yet?"

"Takes a while. Soon, I hope."

"You been at it a while."

"Seems like forever."

Kitty started putting thing away. "Momma send for you?"

She nodded.

"Well, it's my thing. Not yours."

"What happens to you happens to all of us."

"Don't give me that shit. We lives our own lives." Kitty tossed her hair back and forth, long, knotted braids. She appeared more mature physically than she on her last visit.

"What kind of life do you think you're going to live?"

"Kind I want to."

"And what kind is that?"

"Lots of girls has babies afore they gets married."

"You mean around here."

"This is where I live."

"You intend to live in this crumby ghetto all your life?"

"I'm not goin to spend all my life tryin to get a Ph.D."

"How do other those other pregnant girls live?"

"They lives."

"And they all get married to the guys who knocked them up?"

"They ain't all married. So what? Gettin married ain't no big deal. Ricky'll marry me. You'll see."

"Did he say he would?"

"He ain't said nothin yet."

"He knows you're pregnant?"

"I told him."

"What did he say?"

"He said, 'Oh yeah?'"

"Pretty enthusiastic, huh?"

"Shit."

"You can do better than that. Even if he were willing to marry you, how would he support you and your baby?"

"I can get a job."

"Doing what?"

"Somethin'."

"While he takes care of the baby?"

"Momma can take care of the baby."

"When? Momma works all day so the rest of you can eat and have a roof over your head. You're going to take care of all of them with your well-paying job at fifteen?"

"Shit."

"You're worth more than that, Kitty. You're doing well at high school. You're attractive. You don't have to settle for what's available the first time around."

"Not all of us is like you, Vanessa. We don't run off from the rest of us and have fancy ideas 'bout being big shots."

"If you have a fancy idea, you can work to make it happen."

"Won't happen to me. I got what I got."

"Get more."

"I can't."

"You can."

"I b'long here. I'm stuck anyway now."

"You're not stuck."

"I'm pregnant."

"You can have an abortion."

"That's what Ricky said."

"Ricky said that? He wants you to have an abortion?"

"He said he knows somebody."

"You don't go to somebody he knows. You go to a proper doctor. There are clinics."

"I got no money."

"We'll manage. It has to be done properly, under sanitary conditions."

"I don't want to have it done."

"You're just going to let things happen to you? The way you got pregnant?"

"I don't want to do nothing."

"If you just let things happen to you, you end up nowhere. You've got to make decisions. You can't sleepwalk your way through life."

"Van, I'm scared. I don't even want to think about it."

"Do what you have to do, then think about it."

"Easy for you to say."

"I do what I say."

"I'm not you, and I'm scared." Kitty's face squinted into a bitter ball. Tears squeezed from her eyes.

She put her arms around her. "It's all right, baby. You just go through with it. Everybody makes mistakes. You fix them however you can. You hurt and then you go on."

Kitty was sobbing against her shoulder. Vanessa saw her mother's face in the doorway. She shook her head and her mother quickly disappeared.

"I'll go with you. It doesn't take long, but we have to make an appointment. Okay? We'll take care of it, and then we'll talk about what comes next. Would you like to come live with me? I hope I'll have a full time teaching somewhere by the time you graduate from high school. You can to go to college where I teach if you want to. But there's no hurry. One thing at a time. Okay?"

Kitty nodded. She had stopped crying and wiped her face on her sleeve. They went into the living room and Kitty sat on the sofa with her mother. Her mother held her hand.

"I be all right," Kitty said. She leaned her head on her mother's shoulder.

"It's against religion," her mother said. "But sometime you got to get practical."

The sound of the refrigerator door closing caused her mother lift her head as though to hear better.

"Benny? I hear you. No food till supper. Vanessa's here to eat supper with us. You just put it back."

They could hear Benny giggling.

Lila came through the front door and dropped her books on the floor with a crash, and hugged Vanessa. "I didn't know you were coming. You been kicked out of college?"

"Not yet. How's school?"

"Same old shit."

"Lila, don't you use that kind of language in my house."

Lila giggled. "Sorry, Momma. I thought I was in school."

How had she managed them, working all day, her husband off somewhere most of the time and unaccountable? The wonder was that all of them weren't pregnant or drying cars.

"Van, you still studyin to become doctor of literature?"

"Yes."

"What good is literature?"

"Good question."

Lila turned to her mother. "When I passed that house on the corner I saw that dude in the Mercedes again. He's dealin."

"The police won't come when I call," her mother said, shaking her head. "They don't care what goes on in this neighborhood. Did you stop by the library like I told you?"

"Yes, ma'am." Lila reached into her backpack and pulled out a book. The title was plainly visible: *As I Lay Dying.* "Momma and me are going to read it together," she said to Vanessa.

Her mother was doing with Lila what she had done with her, getting her to read and guiding her into the world outside. She had become addicted not to drugs from a dealer in a Mercedes, but to books from the public library, and so she lived other lives and was

70

exposed to ideas she otherwise would never have known about. She had continued to read, a book a day in addition to the books she read for classes, looking up every word she didn't know. Momma, that abandoned, burdened woman, had impelled her out of the ghetto toward another life. She hadn't arrived yet, and she knew now that people were often the same in every world. But she would make it. For Momma. For herself. For all of them.

16 *MICHAEL HORNE*

He woke at five as usual. He decided against running on the seawall. It was already humid and stoking up. He had always awakened at five. He would sip his orange juice and hot tea and read the morning paper while waiting for the children to rise and for Janice and Frieda to tend to them and send them off to their schools. Then he would have a proper breakfast with Janice before leaving for the campus. It had been a good time of day.

He missed his talks with Janice and hearing about her activities and the children's doings. Now he had to ask his children about their lives. When they answered, they selected and sanitized events for his benefit. Except for Mark, they had been friendly at least. Jimmy obviously condescended to professions other than the law, the way M.D.s, having professional degrees, ignorantly condescended to Ph.D.s, but Jimmy was tolerant enough. Laurie was protective and chatty. Their worlds were different and went on at a distance. Gradual euthanasia.

The separation and distance were normal. Was it to be the case with his work as well? His major research had been taken over by others. Did it mean his own contributions were at an end?

He still had research going on in his lab whose directions he had set. And his new interest in ethics, though different, was not exactly an aside. It was another facet of his drive for unambiguous standards for his work.

Coming to Terms

He was not concerned with the theft of ideas, or the politics of competition for federal grants. He was disturbed when he read an article about ethics in science that clearly rooted its arguments in tacit religious assumptions. There ought, he had protested, to be a clear basis for ethics in science that did not rise from tribal *mores,* or religions, or from philosophies like utilitarianism or simple deontology, no matter how attractive or practical they might appear to be. If a code of ethics did not incorporate all the information about human evolutionary biology researchers had uncovered, it would inevitably be arbitrary.

If it was part of his prickly character to oppose ignorance and illogic, it was also inherent in his makeup that he examine his own profession. Scientists were human and subject to their cultural environments. And some were not immune from blind and comforting religious beliefs, not matter how much those beliefs contradicted everything they knew as scientists.

And now there were changes in his life, and consequent changes in his work. His chairmanship of the department had come to an end. And he would be expected give up his research and his work with graduate students and even his lab in five years.

The end of his official scientific activities. He could retire to the Big Sur and tout a vitamin as a panacea like old Linus, but you had to have a Nobel or two to get away with that kind of nonsense. He was serious about his work.

A crisis at seventy? He had suffered other crises in his life. That shaky time he went through when Kennedy was assassinated. While he had a perspective on events of that character now, the effect on him then had been personal and out of proportion. He had acted irrationally to try to deal with it, flying back to Wisconsin as if to turn back time and all that had happened.

He got up from his hot tea and rummaged in his briefcase for his journal. He toted it with him and continued to write in it. It was a kind of reflective history of his life that he could set away from himself and still keep. Had Mark pried into these pages as well the account of Noah's death? 1963.

That long ago?

November 28

73

As usual my mother's letter is full of news about remote relatives and other people I don't know or can't remember. This time she starts off by saying it's the fifth anniversary of my father's "passing." We talk on phone and I send money, but I haven't been back home since my father's death. I can see Zinctown in my mind's eye. It's summer, with driftless green hills and maple trees in full leaf, the air full of birds.

If it is the anniversary of my father's death, then it is almost my birthday. And I don't know who I am. I live in a country that assassinates its president. Was it someone else who lived in Wisconsin with a fanatical father and a subservient mother and easy going friends? When cells replace other cells and the old ones die, do we become different human beings? What have I lost?

November 29

I bought a ticket to Dubuque via Chicago, the only way to get to southwestern Wisconsin. I didn't tell anyone I was going. It was a completely unpremeditated act.

I dozed on the bus from Dubuque to Zinctown and woke up in the neon-lit twilight of fast food shacks along the last half mile into town - all erected since my last visit. Deep fried America. I got off at the Mobil station and U-Haul depot and climbed the hill to Pine in a hash of emotions. Shock at the brand new sleaziness at the edge of town and the sudden view of the old familiar Victorian house where I grew up made me stop.

The house seemed to have shrunk. I stood there for a moment. I walked to the porch. My mother never locked the door, but she wasn't expecting me. The assassination, my nonsensical return to the place I thought I knew that had already receded into the past, made me feel strange, out of my mind. I opened the door and called tentatively: "Mother?"

"Michael?" I heard her voice, disbelieving from the kitchen. I could hear TV voices in the background, the sound of water being turned off, the high clink of a dish. She appeared in the kitchen doorway, wiping her hands on her apron as I crossed the living room. She threw her arms open. I hugged her and patted her on the back. She's still fat, but shorter somehow.

"What are you doing here? Are Janice and the children with

you?" *She was searching around me toward the front door. "Is everything all right? Why didn't you let me know you were coming? I'd have had supper waiting for you."*

"I came by myself. Spur of the moment."

She fell into her characteristic puzzled look. Then she said, "I have some cornbread in the oven and some left-over ham and baked beans. I'll put the ham in the beans and warm them up." She turned toward the kitchen and then back to me. "Is everything all right?"

The television set in the corner of the kitchen was on the news. Cronkite was describing the confusion that still characterized Washington as Lyndon Johnson took over.

"Everything is fine," I said. I tried to think of something to say. I was glad to see her and to be home. There is no confusion here. "You've got a new TV set."

"The old one broke down," she said in the apologetic tone she had always fallen into with my father when something went wrong, even when it was something mechanical over which she had no control. "It's not really new. It's a used one that got fixed." She turned the set off.

She lives in her kitchen, cooking, eating, entertaining her church friends, reading mystery novels, watching baseball games on TV. She follows the Brewers and knows all their batting averages.

As I ate baked beans and ham and cornbread, I was living in the past. She poured me a glass of milk without asking and I was ten again. Even when I wolfed my food down as a kid, eating in my mother's kitchen was a joy. Though I paid no attention, my mother always talked. I heard every word, I realize now, though I would have sworn then that I just ate and tuned out her monologues. There would be approval or disapproval in her tone. Did I learn moral lessons from her tales?

Today she talked about the assassination of the president. It was hard for her to believe such a thing could happen in America. She hadn't voted for Kennedy because he was a Catholic, but she thought he was a good president. And killing him was an evil act. Then she changed the subject. "You look more and more like your father."

I was not pleased to hear it. There was a photograph of my father sitting on the TV, and I gazed at it over my mother's shoulder as she talked and gave me second helpings of everything and butter melted into the cornbread wedges. My father was good-looking enough; it was his character that offended me. He was honest and hard working and frugal, but he was offensive in the way only rigidly pious people can be. The word "dour" was invented to describe him.

God was with him in the mines, and together they dug for doctrine and came up with zinc to make nickels. His fellow miners drank at the Second Street bars and beat each other to death for fun. My father's pleasure was to beat his family to death for religion.

November 30

I slept in my old room last night, in my own bed, with the same photos on the wall, one of them of my high school baseball team. An old suit hangs forlornly in the closet. Sweaters are stacked on the shelf, a baseball glove rests beside them. A bat leans in the corner, and old pair of cleated shoes lies, pigeon-toed, on the floor beneath. My bookcase still holds high school textbooks and Silas Marner.

Does my mother expect me start school again? Atop the bookcase is my grandfather's hunting cap.

At first I had a hard time sleeping. Part of the disorientation I'm going through. It's like a virus. I tossed and turned, asking myself questions like Job, but lacking faith and submission. I refused to accept what had happened. I finally settled down. I told myself I was home again, safe, in my old bed. I slept the way I had when I was young.

I woke to the sun shining through my window the way it used to. I could smell bacon frying. I clomped to the shower. I found clean clothes in my dresser. The Tee-shirt was loose. Have I gotten thinner? I found a shirt, slightly out of date, folded neatly in a drawer.

My mother broke eggs into a skillet when she saw me. She had baked soda biscuits, enough for six, and brought out her home-made strawberry jam. I was surprised at how much I could eat. My mother turned off the TV and talked about my father again.

"Your father really cared about you," she said. She was drinking her black coffee and overseeing my eating.

"That was pretty hard to tell," I said, spreading jam an inch thick on my biscuit.

"He just couldn't express his feelings wanted you to have everything, like a college education."

"He thought what I learned in college was unchristian and he was suspicious of my friends even in high school. He disapproved of my going to parties with my friends where they drank beer."

"He worried about you." My mother's face bore a frown appropriate to my father's worries. "And you know he didn't approve of drinking."

"He wanted me to be educated and still believe in his superstitions and not do anything he wouldn't have done. He wanted me to be weirdo to my fellow students."

"There's lots of educated people who are good Christians. Do you want more bacon?"

"No thanks. "I've already eaten twice as much as I am used to these days." I wiped my face on one of my mother's hand embroidered napkins. I was being treated as a guest. "I'm not a good Christian. People ought to be able to believe what they choose to believe."

"You know he came from a very poor family and they had to work hard to stay alive. He worked hard, too, to give us a decent life. That's what he believed in. That and God's will. He was proud of you. He was proud of your service in Korea. You shouldn't look down on him."

"Look down on him?" I was taken aback. It hadn't occurred to me that I had looked down on him. On the contrary, he had always seemed to be a fearsome giant who towered over my childhood.

"That's what he thought you did, especially toward the end of his life. He gave you everything he could. He sent money when he could when you went away to that university in California. And you looked down on him."

"I didn't look down on him. I didn't disrespect him for working hard. I just had to be myself."

"You made it obvious that you had no use for his religion. I remember the expressions on your face when you argued with him."

"He had no respect for my opinions, or even my right to have them. I felt oppressed by his dogmatic attitudes."

"He wanted to see you before he died, and when it was close, he asked me to call you. It was hard for him to ask, but he did. He was heart-broken when you weren't there when he passed away."

"You know I tried to get back." Why did she bring that up? "There was an ice storm at O'Hare."

"You meant the world to him." My mother shook her head. "The two of you are exactly alike. "Stubborn." She busied herself clearing the breakfast table.

Breakfast had cheered me, but talk about my father had depressed me. The president's assassination and my father's death seem to have gotten spliced in my mind.

Am I like my father? That notion that I should feel guilty amazes me. The belief that I looked down on him is silly. Why is my mother saying all those things? I changed the subject. "What has happened to Ronnie? You mentioned in a letter he was still in town."

"He bought the Gentlemen's Shop from Mrs. Tolliver last year."

"Old Tolliver died and Ronnie is a haberdasher? I think I'll look him up. What happened to Erin Nelson?"

She looked up from the skillet she was scouring. "She's Erin Peterson now. She has two little daughters and teaches art at the elementary school part time. Her husband is Larry Peterson. You remember him? He was a couple of years ahead of you in high school. He inherited the feed mill when his father died."

"I guess I do vaguely. Jimmy and Frank Thomas?"

"Jimmy moved to Colorado. Frank died in a car accident a year ago."

We talked about people I had known. Hearing their names was like waking from a dream. I'm Rip Van Winkle. As I put on my old baseball jacket, I heard the TV go on in the kitchen. My mother has to have talk going on - her own, or somebody else's. I walked to the Gentlemen's Shop.

The town seems smaller, too. A couple people I passed looked vaguely familiar. They glance at me as though they knew me. I nodded. Ronnie has gussied up the front of his shop with Olde English lettering and fake oak. It smells better, too. Like Olde English cologne. Ronnie shouted when he saw me.

"Goddamn! I can't believe it. What are you doing in little old Zinctown? Mike, how are ya?" He seized my hand in his old

*baseball grip and sported a big grin on his face. He looks the same
except for a balding pate. He was wearing a red vest and a red tie.*

"Your pitching arm is as strong as ever," I said, extricating
my hand. "I'm okay. How are you?"

"Fine and dandy, as you can see. And all this is mine. And the
bank's. I bought it from Jane Tolliver when old Henry died."

"So I heard. How's business?"

"Can't complain. Least I'm making the bank payments." He
punched me on my biceps. "And how's California? You still teaching
there?" He shifted his gum to the other cheek.

"Yeah. Research. Same stuff."

"What brings you here? Vacationing?"

"Sort of. Spur of the moment."

"Don't guess I'll ever make it out of here." A crooked grin
pulled at the side of his mouth.

"Why would you want to leave this part of the country?"

"You did, didn't you? It's God's country, but I'd trade you any
day to get to the city. Let's go have coffee at Joe's."

*He went on over coffee, shifting his gum as he talked and sipped.
He had hoped for something bigger and better, but when the chance
came to buy Henry's store, he figured that was it. He had a
bachelor's degree in education, but he didn't like teaching. Molly
was teaching and liked it well enough. Putting their incomes
together, they got along all right. He and Molly still went bowling
Saturday nights. They bought a new camper and planned to drive
to Eagle Lake for a couple of weeks in the summer. He still liked
hunting and fishing. They went to Eagle Lake last summer with
Larry and Erin Peterson. Maybe he be able to swing a buying trip
to New York. He'd sure like to have one good fling in his life.* "You
remember Erin?" He grinned.

"How is Erin?"

"Looks pretty good for her age. She still paints. She had a
show at the library last year. Larry doesn't think too much of it, I
guess, but he puts up with her idiosyncrasies. The feed mill does
pretty well, as it always has. Probably the best business in town."

*What am I doing here, listening to Ronnie? I came back to my
roots in a kind of reflex action, and this is what I find. Are these my
roots? What has become of the green hills and my nostalgic*

memories of southwest Wisconsin? Ronnie suggested we get together with some of our old championship baseball team, but I begged off saying I had to get back. He punched me on my biceps and said he'd look me up if he ever got to the west coast.

There had been no mention of the assassination. What had I hoped to find that would make steady what had been thrown into chaos?

I walked the familiar streets, past bare maple trees, the dime store, the bank, the photography studio, the gift shop, the hardware store, pick-up trucks, men wearing caps with long bills bearing a logo for Peterson's Feed Mill. I can't stay for this. And I don't want to go back.

When I returned to the house my mother said Janice had called to report I was missing. She was surprised to learn I was in Zinctown. My mother was surprised Janice didn't know where I was. My office had called Janice about me. I should call Janice. I should call my office. Everybody is worried about me. I am worried about me.

"Spur of the moment." I said.

"Is something wrong?"

Yes, I wanted to say. With me. With America.

"I just had to get away for a day or so. I should have told Janice."

My mother shook her head, mystified. "Erin Peterson called, too."

"How did she know I was here?"

"News travels fast in Zinctown."

"What did she want?"

"Didn't say."

"I'll call her later."

"She said you should call right away."

I called her. "Michael?" Her voice sounded the same, though I had forgotten how Midwestern she sounded. I must have sounded that way when I lived in Zinctown. We went through the usual greetings. She asked what I was doing home. I gave my evasive answer. She wanted to see me. She had to go out early in the evening, but she would stop by about eight thirty and take me for a drink.

"With Larry?"

"Don't be silly. You two don't know each other."

I told my mother I would be going out later that evening. She bestowed her suspicious expression on me.

I remember it from way back. I said I was tired and was going to take a nap. In fact, I was groggy. I fell sleep at once and didn't wake until dark, an awful dream winding through my head about being lost in an endless corridor like the high school corridor of my youth, not knowing what time it was and which class I should be going to next. The dream was rooted in high school when the bell would ring while I was in study hall and I was in a dungeon with the Count of Monte Cristo (Dumas inside the geography text I was supposed to be reading), and I would wake to Zinctown High and not know where I was. It was seven thirty after I added two hours to my watch. I felt groggier than when I went to sleep. I took a brisk shower, trying to wake up. My mother had saved supper for me. I wasn't hungry, but I had no desire to offend her. Even hot apple pie didn't revive my spirits. I called Janice. She was baffled. No matter what I should have called.

My mother was listening to a football game in the distance as I sat in the parlor thinking of my dream and the fears of my childhood. Once my shoe got caught in the crotch of a maple tree. The week before I had climbed to the level of the second story window from which my mother saw me waving and had become frightened. My father ordered her to remain calm while he came to the tree and ordered me to climb down. He had beaten me with a razor strop and warned me not to climb the tree again. Now my shoe had trapped me. I decided to wait until the man who lived next door returned from work to ask for help. He was a friend who supplied me with dimes for ice cream cones and gum. He rescued me but reported it to my father. I didn't know then that adults who are friends of children betray them to parents.

What I remember on my own is my shoe being stuck and the texture of the bark and the ants crawling into cracks in the bark and being beaten with a razor strop and being rescued by my neighbor from the tree. The rest is a family story.

I heard a horn and saw a vehicle at the curb. I put on my baseball jacket and told my mother I wouldn't be late. How many times did I say that when I was young? The vehicle was a pick-up truck with a camper on the back.

"You're driving a pick-up truck?"

"Well, I'm picking you up, aren't I?"

As she put the truck through gears, I examined her in the lights from the dashboard and the street lamps. Her hair style is different; it use to hang half-way down her back. It's the same thick black. She is still willowy, with a long, exotic face. Her father owned a jewelry store on Main, and they lived in a brick house farther down on Main. They were higher class than my mining family, but her mother liked me. Michael will go a long way, she used to say.

"Do I pass inspection?" Erin said. We were speeding along County M into rolling farm land. The hills were dark and a flurry of snow began to fall on the windshield. I could smell damp earth through the vents.

"As pretty as ever," I said.

She reached for my hand and squeezed it. Then she placed both hands on the wheel and swerved into the Rosedale Cemetery.

"Rosedale?" I said.

"Yep. Lovers' Lane, remember?" She laughed and stopped the truck at the end of the access road.

"I thought you were taking me for a drink."

"Right." She reached back of her seat and brought out a bucket in which a bottle of champagne was surrounded by ice cubes. We laughed.

"Glasses in the glove compartment," she said.

The glasses were wrapped in a towel. I unwound them as she pushed on the cork until it popped. I held out the glasses. She filled them carefully to the brim and stuck the bottle back into the bucket. I handed her a glass and she laughed again, her eyes aglow in the faint light. We clinked and our glasses and drank.

"I've waited a long time for you to come back," she said.

"It's been a long time," I said. My stomach fluttered. What other surprises did she have planned? And what did she mean? We had fun in Rosedale when we were in high school, with illegal beer, not champagne. "My mother has been keeping me up to date."

"I can understand why you haven't come back with all there is to do in Berkeley and San Francisco. I tried to persuade Larry to take a trip to the west coast three years ago, but he wasn't interested.

Are you still at Berkeley?" Her thigh was warm against mine.

"I'm there for life, I guess. I have tenure."

"I'm still painting, but I'm stymied." She filled our glasses again. "Nobody here appreciates art, or anything cultural, for that matter, except a few people at the college. I can't move ahead because I don't talk to other painters, or see what they're doing. I need to get to a big city. I keep dreaming about going to New York, anywhere there are galleries and artists. It must be great for you at Berkeley."

"I can understand," I said. The champagne was getting to me. She was topping off our glasses again. Snow was coming was coming down in earnest and the windows were fogging.

"I missed you so much when you went away. I kept thinking you'd come back for me." She put her glass on the dash.

"What about Larry?"

"He's a nice enough guy, and a good father, but business is everything. He likes art if it features naked women or hunting and fishing scenes." She shivered. "I'll get a blanket from the back."

The snow was blowing hard and the cold wind blew in the door when she opened it. She brought a blanket to the front and drew it over us.

"We used to say we belonged to each other," she said.

"That was a long time ago," I said. "We were high school kids. All those promises we made took place in another life. We were different people."

"Take me back with you," she said suddenly. "We can start where we left off when you went away." She pounded me on the chest. "I've got to get out of here. I'm thirty years old and I'm dying."

"I can't," I said. "I have a wife and three kids. And you have a husband and two daughters." The assassination had thrown me off balance. I couldn't accept it. And now Erin wanted to take me back to the past. I couldn't go back. I couldn't go on either. And she was another person, the self she had become in all the years she had lived.

"I'll do anything. I'll get a job. I can't stand Larry anymore."

"What about your daughters?" It was crazy. The snow and the fog of our breath that had whitened out the windows as we sat

there in the cold cab of her pick-up made her proposal seem even more unreal.

"I'll take them with me if I have to. Can't you understand? My life is just down hill. I'm sliding into Rosedale in a hearse minute and after minute. Help me stay alive." She clutched my arm as though she were drowning.

I'm thirty and I came back to Zinctown. Erin is thirty and she wants out of Zinctown. Thirty is everywhere. The Count of Monte Cristo is gone, and there is the geography book.

"I can't do it," I said. "I'm dying myself. I hate California." My own anguish was catching up to me.

"You can't hate yourself. You can't hate California." She had pinned her hopes of escape on me. The snow and darkness had closed us off completely. We were in the same space but separate worlds, talking past each other in our private soliloquies. "Michael, Michael, is everything impossible?"

She was crying, and clinging to my arm. I felt tears on my own face. Something had let go. I had drunk too much champagne. I fought down the anguish that rose from somewhere deep, from the damp earth, the graves around us. I was grieving for Zinctown, for California, for my father, my mother, my wife, my kids, my high school sweetheart, my president, myself. We were trapped in time gone by, in selves that had gone by. My soul was caught in the crotch of a tree.

He closed his journal, resting his hands on it, as though he had closed a book on life. The binding was splitting along the edges. The paper was turning yellow. His mother had died fifteen years ago. Erin had gone off to New York a year after their tryst, leaving her daughters behind with Larry. He had lost track of her. Did it matter that they had huddled together, drunk, under a blanket in a snow storm in the middle of a cemetery all years ago? He had relived his account of his wonted contention between father and son. If his own son read his account of his irrational return to Zinctown, what would he have made of it?

And now he faced the conclusion of his professional life. When the time comes, his grandfather had said, put me in a pine box and put my hunting cap on top.

17 *LEAH STEIN*

The illuminated dial read 12:01. She couldn't tell whether it was midnight or noon. She closed her eyes again. She didn't care. Pulses of pain rose and fell at the back of her head. She opened her eyes again and saw light slipping between the edges of the drapes and the wall. Noon. Her mouth tasted liked sour milk. She remembered she wanted to die.

She wanted to cry but she was too sick to cry. She longed to reach a state of oblivion, to escape from pain. From herself. She closed her eyes but they opened again on their own. There was an empty glass beside the clock. She was dehydrated, but the thought of swallowing something made her feel sicker.

Beside the glass was an old *Glamour*, the magazine Lydia had subscribed to. All those skinny women trying to be sleek and sexy with expensive clothes and thick makeup, and being brave about being female and choosing the right male. Being successful on the job while being female. Coping with yeast infections and urinary tract infections and toxic syndromes and worrying about herpes and HIV, yet being attractive and sexy to Mr. Right. Being female on glossy paper. What did it mean to Lydia now?

I am still alive, Lydia, but I am not young and sleek. I'm no longer attractive to males even when I throw myself at them.

I belong with my clients. Fuck them all. That was what Mark

had said the last time they were together. She hadn't known it would be the last time. They had gone to a movie at the Park, the little restaurant in Hillcrest, the bookstore, the bakery where they always went for cheesecake. It was going to be a different kind of evening, but how could she have known? They talked politics.

"All politicians are liars but Bush has been the worst. The whole basis for the war was phony. There were no weapons of mass destruction. The tiny fifth-rate country on the other side of the globe was no immanent threat. Has he started a war that will never end? He was determined to go to war with Iraq the moment he took office because, as he said, they tried to kill his daddy. And look what his goons are doing to the Constitution."

His face had turned red. His pale blue eyes, set deep in his head, glared like klieg lights at the scene of a crime.

It was his anger at the establishment that had first drawn her to him. He had always aired his opinions with a conviction that was more than intellectual. And some of the group at UCSD had been frightened at his intensity. He had been in the reserves and got called and sent to Iraq. Why had he been in the reserves? It was an inexplicable inconsistency.

Some of their group had predicted he would mellow once he got the job at UCSD, but he had not. He had refuse to serve on the editorial board of *Verso, the Left Hand Page,* when they asked him, but he donated money. And so did Lydia. The magazine had a small circulation, mostly at places like Berkeley and Wisconsin. He drove around in his old Volvo, helping to distribute it to bookstores and coffee shops. Others in the group thought he was demented, a revolutionary but a nerd. He didn't smoke pot or even drink.

She finished her wine. "Do you want to come back to Lydia's house? She was talking yesterday about our days as students at UCLA. She'd like to see you, if she's still awake."

"Why don't they just let her die?" he said. Why the fuck are they keeping her alive? Are they trying to prove something?"

"They have her on pain-killing drugs. It's a tricky business, even with all the publicity about the right to die."

"Can't she do it herself? How does she take the drugs?"

"Injection. It's difficult for her to swallow, so can't take them by mouth."

"Who gives them to her?"

"Whoever is there with her. I'm there mornings and at night."

"Why don't you give an overdose?"

"Oh, no. I couldn't do that."

"Why not?"

"I don't have the courage. Besides, they would do an autopsy and find out. Could you do that?"

"I did it once." His face had gone angry again. He stared at her. He was in his maniacal mood.

"In Iraq?"

"He was all shot up and we had to pull out. He was paralyzed and bleeding from his legs and his guts. We had too many wounded we were trying to take with us. He asked me to finish him off. If he had stayed alive even for a little while, the Iraqis would have tortured him. Jesus Christ."

Tears suddenly streamed down his face and he put his head on his arms. His shoulders were heaving. She put her hand on his arm tentatively. She had never seen him this way. The tough guy attitudes, the sarcasms, the dictionary of angers all dissolved in spasms.

In a few minutes, he blew his nose in a paper napkin and said, "Let's get out of here."

As he drove, he recovered. The customary controlled spleen with which he drove came back. He cursed drivers who got in his way or made illogical moves. When they reached Lydia's house, he turned off the engine and sat, head down.

She waited. She couldn't tell whether he wanted her to get out and go in the house, or whether he wanted to go in, or just sit there. She didn't dared ask. She rested her hand on his arm, hoping for a sign. She couldn't think of anything to say.

"My father killed a man once. He was dying of cancer. He was my godfather."

"Did he tell you?"

"I read it in his journal," he said

"How did he kill him?"

"With a gun. Noah wanted to kill himself, but he couldn't do it because he didn't have enough strength. My father pushed Noah's hand on the trigger."

She could see tears glistening in the street light.

"I loved Noah. He was gentle and believed in saving everything that lived, like plants and animals. He worked to keep them from being extinguished by humans. My mother was gentle, too, like Noah. People don't care about living things. If they wanted to have peace, we wouldn't have wars. People kill. Everything. Animals, humans. The planet."

"Not everybody."

"Everybody. For whatever reason. For political reasons. For religious reasons. For reasons of possession. For sport. Take your pick. The reasons change and disappear. The dead are dead."

"Did you kill in Iraq?"

"Iraq is only a symptom. History. A black stone wall in Washington with names on it tells you that the dead are dead. You do it and it never lets go. In Iraq the enemy was everywhere. Be a martyr and go to heaven where there's plenty of booze and girls. It's Bush's official policy not to pay attention to the dead when they come home."

He had never talked this way before, and she didn't dare spoil it by saying the wrong thing. He needed to talk. It wasn't exactly rational, but she longed to know what he felt. It scared her. Was this the real Mark, or was it only another layer? What was still hidden? Maybe he was just using her.

"You think wars bring out what's already there?"

"You find out what's inside you. Civilization is a thin membrane over savagery. We're tribes surrounded by other tribes."

"You had friends in Iraq."

"To survive. We had to rely on each other. All we had was each other. That's civilization."

Light from the corner lamp caught the side of his face as he turned away. He looked like a cadaver. "I'm doing something for them."

"How?" Maybe she shouldn't ask.

"I can't tell you."

"Do you want to come in?"

"No. If you want to go in, that's okay."

"I want to be with you."

"What I said about Iraq is a lie."

She withdrew her hand from his arm.

"I'm sorry. I didn't mean to hurt your feelings."

They sat. He had never said so much about his feelings. What he said had changed her understanding of him. Was it closer to his real self? He might regret having said so much. He might be resentful of her.

He said he had to go. "Fuck 'em all," he said. This time he seemed to say it sadly, as though he had given up on the rest.

She fell asleep and woke with a start. She was dizzy. She went to the bath and drank a glass of water. She drank slowly lest she be sick, and went back to bed, hovering between nausea and exhaustion. If she had known what Mark would do, what could she have done? He talked about Iraq and then said he lied. Had he really killed a wounded fellow soldier? She couldn't believe he would say all that if it were really a lie. Yet she couldn't believe he would do it. Then why did he say it? Had his father actually killed someone? He hadn't mentioned Noah before. Had the things he said been signs of what he might do? Or did they mean something else? She sat on the edge of the bed. Still dizzy.

Screwy and full of unrooted anger as he was, she had loved him. And she had loved gentle Lydia. They were dead.

And Orin had rejected her. She must have been deranged to try to claim whatever it was she wanted from him. To be accepted, To take Lydia's place. She had to stop conning herself. She had to give up hope of being someone other than who she was.

First, she had to get out of this house.

18 *LUPE VIDA*

The world was upside down. The sky was dark and the stars were shining up from the earth The dark sky reflected the light of the earth's stars.

"That is the City of the Angels," José said.

The city seemed endless and it frightened her. "It is time to stop," she said. "No one will give us a ride after dark."

She held Juanito closer to her breast. It would be cold at night again. She wrapped the baby in the blanket and covered his head with the end of the blanket like a cowl. She had doubled the blanket but it was still much too big for the baby. It was the only warm thing they had. They had taken it from the bedroom of the house the kind old man let them stay in until she was able to walk. They all slept under it at night.

They had been given rides in cars and trucks when people saw the baby. The Anglos would want to see the baby. The Mexicans would warn them about the *migras*. One man said some illegals were returning to Mexico because the big ranchers were afraid to hire them. But José said he still had hope.

María Josefa, her cousin on her mother's side had written to tell them about Los Angeles. She said if they decided to come, she and José could stay with them until José found a job and they could find a place of heir own to live. But housing was expensive, even in Mexican ghettos, and the rents were so high. She had read the letter to José.

José said he wanted to think about it. Then, in the morning, he said: "*Bien.* I will go, but it would be difficult for you because of your condition. I will send for you when I have a job."

"The baby is not due yet," she said. "I'm going with you. I do not want to be separated from you. I wish to be with you when Juanito is born."

"*Bien.* But it may be Teresa, not Juanito." They laughed together. She knew José hoped it would be a boy.

María Josefa and her husband lived with her brother and their family in the small house. They were also illegals. Her brother had lived in Los Angeles for five years.

They had hope, but the size and strangeness of the city upset her. They had reached hills where they could Los Angeles. Juanito was strong and sucked well and cried only when he was hungry or uncomfortable or too warm in the day or too cold in the night. He would be handsome and strong like José. And like her father. She hoped they could make enough money to send some American dollars to her father. He had no money and lived with her sister. Her sister's husband was not happy to have him living with them because he didn't have much money himself. He had worked for a big ranch in the valley until he was too old. She prayed for him every night. They would return to their village with enough money to farm her father's *ejido*, or they would find a place in the city of stars.

The city confused her. The millions of cars always moving, the noise, the smog, the endless people. In her village people knew each other. Here she knew only María Josefa and the people in the house. Seven people in the small house with two bedrooms. José gave María Josefa some of the money the old man had given them. She cried at night after José fell asleep. Juanito kept waking and crying. José could do only farm work. He was not trained to do anything else. He went out where María Josefa's husband told him to go, into fields where vegetables were grown. They did not look like farmlands. They were fields that waited for houses that all looked alike to be built on them. The farms were irrigated and the farmers had fine machinery. But the lettuce had to be picked by hand.

It was not a city of stars or angels. It was like the inferno that Father Jorge had described in his sermons. What would happen to Juanito if he grew up here? She wished to go home, but there was no work at home. She crossed herself and wiped her eyes. Juanito began crying. She opened her dress and gave him a nipple. He made noises and sucked. Save Juanito, she prayed. Juanito's hand found the little cross that hung from her neck. Her father had given her the cross for her confirmation. Juanito pulled at it and then let it go. She stroked his head until he fell asleep.

19 *JIMMY HORNE*

The morning paper was fat with photographs of the storm's usual drastic effects all the way from Santa Cruz to Mendocino County: power lines down, homes sliding into ravines as the muddy slopes gave way, beach houses canted into the tide, the stunned dispossessed, strained "officials" pressed to make preliminary estimates of damage.

Jimmy found his route through debris to his office, where, thank God, he found electricity on and the elevators working. He had to arrive before his first client of the day, an early riser, got there from Marin County, and whose path to the city no storm would dare obstruct. Bill Koch, the newspaper tycoon, aged eighty-five, was hinting again about making a will that would arrange his retirement and the succession of his media empire.

"Should I be satisfied at having stayed the execution of my fate? I should retreat to my estate with my housekeeper, my gardener, and my chauffeur, and let others take over, and live, however long or briefly, with my memories? Despite how politely they say it, it's what they wish I would do."

Still possessed of his acid wit, Koch paced his office like a caged tiger in the San Diego zoo the moment Jimmy's secretary had shown him into the office.

"Retire, leave my newspapers, televisions stations, buildings, investments to somebody else? You can't imagine, Jimmy, what that's asking of me."

"It's smarter to arrange for all that yourself than to let it get dragged through litigation for years and eventually split up in ways you would not have preferred."

"I'm eighty-five. My doctor sees signs and hears sounds that tell him my time is not long. I don't need him to warn me. I can add. He thinks I should quit. Quit what? They would like me to hand over the power. Power, you known damn well, is all there is. Do you have some coffee?"

He moved to his bar where water was boiling. He poured water over freshly ground French Roast beans and bore the steaming cup to Koch who had seated himself on the sofa. He sometimes thought that his coffee was why Koch kept him on a retainer.

Koch sipped the coffee with a mmm of satisfaction. Then he put on a rueful face. "I have come under false pretenses. I'm not ready to decide about my will. I came about something else. I need confidential advice and counsel."

"That's what you pay me for," Jimmy said. He waited patiently while Koch sipped and decided how to he was going to tell his attorney what the issue was about. A self-made man of the old fashioned sort, sophisticated and simple minded at the same time. Koch placed his cup on the coffee table in front of him. "My friends in Washington tell me I'm being investigated."

"By whom? For what?"

"I don't know the answer to either question, for certain."

"How do you know, exactly?"

"A friend, a columnist who has an inside track to the White House, tells me this is what he was told."

"He was told to leak that to you?"

"That's the way it works. Then my accountant told me that someone got a court order to look at my financial records."

"That could be the IRS."

"And some federal agents are asking questions at my bank."

"What's the condition of the bank?"

"Well, we invest in a lot of different kinds of things. Recently we bought a ton of shares in a technical outfit. Silicon Valley kind of stuff. Venture capital with a chance of making a good deal of money. With Pete Webster. He said the market in these things was far below what it ought to be, and it was a good time for us to get in."

"And?"

"You lose some and you win some."

"I thought Webster declared bankruptcy last year. Where did he get the money?"

"I had the bank lend him some money on a private basis."

"And how did that go?"

"I had the bank reschedule the loan."

"Is the amount enough to affect liquidity?"

"I'm the majority stockholder. I shifted some money."

He waved his hand vaguely. "But then my company put some money two years ago into a reserve account, so we could even out our income, you know. Income varies from years to year, of course, and we wanted to keep our profits on an even keel."

"And the stocks stay high."

"Yeah, well, that's the whole idea. We didn't disburse it. We just held it."

"And you didn't pay taxes on it the years you earned it, and then you changed records again when you put it back in to keep stock values high."

"It all evens out."

"But, of course, the tax amount is different. Isn't there a legitimate way of doing that sort of thing?"

"I don't know."

"Neither do I. But it's clear you've got the IRS and the banking sleuths both on your tail. We've got a genius on these matters on our staff, and I'm going to put her onto this stuff. You'll have to give her complete access to everything."

"Okay."

"Is that it?"

"They've been checking on money I've been sending to foreign banks."

"Where?"

"Luxembourg."

"Why have you been depositing money in Luxembourg?"

"I did it first back when Reagan was president to help the

Freedom Fighters after Congress cut their balls off. The money was transferred to a Contra account."

"The Statute of Limitations has run out on the Freedom Fighter bit, I'm sure. You said first of all."

"Well, there's there still Cuba."

"Cuba?"

"It's still a commie country."

"You're sending money to some Freedom Fighter outfit that's trying to overthrow Castro?"

"Goddamn right. He's a terrorist, isn't he?"

"How are you doing that?"

"We're making sure they get arms and supplies."

"You're arranging for them to secure arms?"

"You can't get rid of that bastard unless you shoot him."

Jimmy went to the bar and fixed himself a cup of coffee. He could really use a good stiff scotch, he thought. He sipped his coffee carefully. "I'm pretty sure the Nicaragua stuff is out from under the law. And I don't know which federal agency, if it is a federal agency, might be interested in you. The supplying of arms to any group might get you into trouble with somebody."

Koch sagged. He had been hyper and defiant, but now the wind had gone out. "Give me another cup of your coffee. My doctor says don't drink more than one cup a day, but will he live as long as I have?"

He took Koch's cup and poured another. Koch accepted it and sank back into the pillows.

"Where are these rebels located?"

"I don't know for sure. I don't ask. Miami probably."

"I don't know what kind of trouble you may be in about depositing money in foreign banks that's being used in arms activity. As I remember there were drug connections in the Nicaragua case. Maybe that's the factor here without your knowledge. But setting up armed activities could be a problem."

He set his cup on the bar. "We have connections in Washington and I'll try to find out what's known and perhaps illegal, if anything, about this Freedom Fighter activity. You're going to have to give me all the information you have. Don't send any e-mails or make any telephone calls to anyone. Your fellow activists, your bank in

Luxembourg, anyone at all. And it's not only the government you have to be concerned about. If Castro knows about you and what you're doing, you could be in danger."

"All right. I'm in your hands." Koch finished his forbidden second cup. "I knew your grandfather on your mother's side, you know. He was a real bastard. Utterly ruthless. Not like your mother."

"So you've told me."

"I trust you, Jimmy. I rely on you to get these sonsabitches off my back. And if you decide to go into politics, you know you can count on my support." He lowered his cup shakily to the coffee table and struggled to rise. He had regained his old age as he shook hands and shuffled to the door.

Jimmy accompanied him and opened the door.

"I wish I had a son like you," Koch said.

How could a hard-nosed old entrepreneur like Koch let himself get caught up in such shenanigans? He was shrewd but naive. It was one thing to hold conservative views; it was radical and dangerous to skirt the law to promote them.

With a Scotch-on-the-rocks, now that his client had gone, he walked to the window. The tower was tall enough to afford a panoramic view of the city and the bay - and to be a tempting target for a plane loaded with gasoline. His great grandfather had owned a chunk of the waterfront he could encompass in his view. The whole family had been involved in shipping in the days before planes existed. His great-uncle Aaron had spent time in jail for smuggling opium from China. Koch was caught in changing times. You needed political finesse as well as a capacity for ruthlessness. They were all passé.

Koch had had a reputation as a womanizer in his day. Jimmy envied the freedom he enjoyed. His own affairs were more discreet, conducted without bravado. A rendezvous in a motel once a week was hardly romance in the grand style. "You're a sybarite not a Casanova," Marie had shouted at him. When he regarded himself honestly, he acknowledged she was right. She understood him better as a critic than she as a wife. When she found out about his "cheating" she exploded. He had been relieved in a way. And saddened because of his daughter.

He left his glass in the sink of his office bar. In the end, Marie had surprised him with the depth of her anger. "Every time you drive a car, I hope you wreck. Every time you fly on a plane, I hope it crashes. Every time you win a case, I hope the losing client blows you away. Every time you fuck somebody's wife, I hope the husband dismembers you." He had never heard her so eloquent, so funny, or seen her so possessed by passion. Were her bitter indignation and wild humor the obverse side of the affection she had once felt for him? He hadn't known her at all.

Perhaps he was blind to the nature of women. He understood business, politics, the law: there were always trade-offs. Surely personal lives were like that. Living was negotiation.

And odd principles, and whimsy. Koch had also had a messy family life. He had disowned his "floozy" daughter, her drug habits, her unpaid bills on Rodeo Drive. And he had disowned his son, "a pot-bellied fifty-year-old Marxist." That was only in his mind. He'd better make a careful will, because the empire he had arduously, if nefariously, erected over the years would collapse.

Koch said he would support him if he went into politics. Would he give up his private life for the fishbowl of Sacramento or Washington? Privacy in office had been the rule for Kennedy, but by the time of Clinton it no longer existed. Muscular governors were used to the living in public, not even worried about their groping reputations. But the reporters would nose around. They all worked for the *Enquirer* in their own newspapers.

He preferred his grandfather's kind of power. He remembered Balzac from his French class: Behind every great fortune there was a great crime. He smiled.

Clara poked her head in the door. "Your daughter is on the phone."

"Linda?"

"Daddy, I'm in the spring play at the college this Friday. Are you coming?"

"Is your mother going to be there?"

"You don't have to sit together."

"I'll be there. I promise."

"I love you, Daddy."

"I love you, Linda."

He hated to face Marie again, but he couldn't let Linda down.

It was all stupid.

The sky was clear after the storm. Did he desire a great fortune? What good had it done Koch, now at the end of his time. No son or daughter to carry on. Was that a necessary part of living a good life? What could anybody leave anybody?

He understood the realities: power, possession, the satisfaction of need and desire. Was there anything beyond them? He doubted it.

20 MICHAEL HORNE

He woke with a start. He had been dreaming he was surrounded by thousands of dead people he didn't know. He could hear rain thwacking the roof. He heard thunder and the dark sky in his window lit up momentarily in a ghostly glow. He was sweating. It was hot. He threw off the sheet that covered him. Probably the electricity had been knocked out and the air conditioning system was not working. He tried to get comfortable against the heat, his usual bony pain, the dregs of his dream.

He remembered Janice waking from a nightmare. She had been dreaming she was falling endlessly through space. She had shaken until his arms around her let her be still. She told him about her dream and insisted that the spirits of the dead were warning her.

"There are no spirits," he said. "And what would they warn you of, if there were? You just had a bad dream. You're all right now."

"I don't want to die."

"You're quite alive. I'm alive. I'm here. The children are here, alive in their rooms." In these moments Janice seemed more vulnerable than she usually did.

"But we will die. You won't be here to say I'm alive and you're alive and the children are alive. It's going to happen."

"Yes, it's going to happen. But we all have this wonderful

meantime. And you have your religion."

"Our bodies die."

"Yes."

"I don't want my body to die."

"Think how you would look at two hundred."

"Don't make fun of me, Michael."

He brushed her hair from her face and kissed her eyes. "Just a little funny to make you think. I'll love you even more when you're two hundred."

"You'll be two hundred, too. Will I love you?"

"I'll probably be even more curmudgeonly."

"Then maybe I won't. You're all I can stand now."

"Maybe you should start looking for someone else now, while you're still young and beautiful and sexy."

She snuggled against him. "I couldn't stand someone else even more."

They laughed together, and he held her until she fell asleep, again.

Confusing the symbolic with the real, Janice believed in "resurrection." He had told her about salmon climbing their native streams, spawning in the headwaters and dying, and about the young salmon coming downstream, the "resurrection" of their progenitors, a continuum that began with the first living cells on earth.

"I'm not a fish," she said. She believed her consciousness would resurrect. She would be there, somewhere, as the self she knew when she woke some thousands of years hence and time had ended.

But without time she would be unconscious, because consciousness consisted of perceptions of events taking place in time. And of events and images constantly being created in the imagination and in memory. Taking place required time. And what of the past inherent in the species, in the chains of reproducing cells? The future kept rising from it, programmed, contingent, subject to mutations, the accidents of environment, catastrophic events. The cells that comprised Janice continued in her in her children and her granddaughter. She had been a moment's constituency of them. Her "self" had vanished and the chain of beings continued.

Though she had hoped to the point of desperate belief that her particular consciousness would survive to resurrect on that impossible and astonishing day to go on forever in some sort of aura of light, she must have had some apprehension of her survival in the unselfconscious cells and their codes in Mark and Jimmy and Laurie. It was fortunate that she had not known of Mark's suicide. Had she sensed that he might, childless, cut himself off from the stream of the living?

She knew about her history, about that tribe of piratical merchants for whom she had, in the end, little use. Her serenity through her life, save for that fearful night of doubt and anxiety, was as much a part of her intuition as it was part of the religion that informed her life, and that she believed, in innocent faith, was the truth of the world.

The rain crashed against the windows in gusts. In noisy bursts of light he could see the branches of live oaks whipping and ducking in a frenzy. The street would be flooded. There was not enough elevation from the gulf and the bay for a storm to drain away before the curbs were awash. As he fell asleep, the storm ebbing in his consciousness, he felt again the strangeness of his being here on this low, sandy island on the Gulf of Mexico, of Mark's death, of the declension of his professional life. Sometimes, like Noah, he wished he could see through the cracks of time into something else.

21 *VANESSA PARSONS*

Hot tea and toast, running on the beach, trying to keep slender, watching the inhabitants of the world on TV slaughtering each other, drug busts, home runs, celebrities changing bed partners, charismatic evangelists fucking prostitutes and conning their gullible disciples out of their savings, sold-out politicians lying piously. And Larry. It was running on the beach that had gotten her Surfboard Larry.

She had to get rid of him. She been taken in by his bronzed body and sun bleached hair, amused by his determined ignorance; but her amusement had begun to erode like sand under a beach house. She finished her tea and sagged. She was falling into a funk.

Her notes, scattered on her desk, told the story. It would take a year to research all the sources and reconstruct the connecting pattern of references she had so cleverly devised. She should have printed out everything as she went along. As she was learning how to use the computer, her instructor had said: Save every little thing every few minutes. She had thought he was paranoid. It was she who was crazy, trusting the computer and trusting Mark. Maybe she should give it up, go ABD, and find the best job she could with a community college, teaching bonehead English. She'd have to get "certificated."

The phone rang. She would tell Larry to stick his surfboard up his honky kazoo. It wasn't Larry.

"Come and see me." Hans said.

"Did you find it?"

"Just come and see me."

"Don't torture me, Hans. It's too important."

"Come and see me, Vanessa."

She pulled off her sleeping shirt, put on a blouse and jeans and sandals, grabbed her purse, and took off for the computer center.

Hans was waiting in his office. His fat German face and pig eyes weren't smiling. He was too discreet to move into Mark's office, playing it cool while the search for Mark's successor got underway.

He handed her a printout. She read it. It didn't make any sense.

"What in hell is this?"

"Read every third line."

"These are pieces of my dissertation!" she shouted. "What's going on? What is the rest of this stuff?"

"Dr. Bergman's research."

"What happened? Can I get my stuff back?"

"Let's go have as cup of coffee."

Hans put his finger on his plump lips, stood and beckoned. She followed. He walked three paces ahead of her, not turning until they were under the eucalyptus trees.

"Now?" she said.

He pointed to the little cafe in the cellar of the next building.

She tagged after him into the cafe and down the line. Hans bought three Danish and a large coffee. She bought tea. They sat at a table in far corner apart from students having breakfast to rap on the sound system.

Hans took a bite from his first Danish and leaned toward her. "Now," he said through his chewing, "let me try to explain."

"I'm waiting." She had always disliked him, and having to watch him eat did not enhance his image in her mind.

"Have some coffee, and don't stare at me so goggle eyed."

"I can't help it." She sipped her tea.

"I'm talking to you here because I don't want anyone at the center to listen in."

"Who in the fuck would want to listen in to a discussion about my computer stuff on novels?"

"It's not your data I'm concerned about."

"Dr. Bergman's data?"

"No. Just keep quiet and listen. And keep your voice down and please don't use that kind of language. Why do you use it, anyway."

"It helps me cope with bastards like you."

He glared at her, then bit into his second Danish. He washed down the Danish with a gulp of coffee. "Your dissertation and Dr. Bergman's research and something else are interleaved, as it were, into a single document. I found out when Dr. Bergman began printing out some of his data. He discovered the mess you saw and came to me." Hans took another bite and signaled to Vanessa to drink up.

She drank up.

"The third line of data mixed up with yours and Dr. Bergman's data seems to have been hacked from files at the Pentagon."

"What?"

"Keep your voice down. It appears that Mark managed to hack into DOD computer files. He disguised the DOD files very simply by mixing them with your files and Dr. Bergman's files. He could access them through Dr. Bergman's file. Dr. Bergman hadn't accessed this particular file for a long time, and Mark probably assumed it was old stuff he wasn't using."

Hans was warning her with his eyes to stay quiet.

"Ah," she said.

"I haven't got the stuff separated yet. I'll have to write a program to do that. It's too difficult to read the way it is."

"What about the DOD? Won't they discover somebody has gotten into their files?"

"Maybe eventually, but it might take them a little longer to figure out who did the breaking in."

"What will happen when they do?"

"Something drastic, I'm sure."

"Mark's dead. What can they do? Take back his purple heart?"

"Don't you get it?" It's what they can do to us, our federal dollars. We do a lot of stuff on federal grants. They might very well take punitive measures. The university stands to lose millions.

Think of the effect on faculty and research projects."

"That sounds pretty heavy. How would they find out?"

"For one thing, by somebody being a blabbermouth."

"You think I'm a rat?"

"You might be by telling a close friend. Remember, I have your dissertation." Hans wiped the last crumbs from his shirt and swigged the last dregs of his coffee. "You have to understand that in the complicated process of separating the three kinds of data from each other, something could get lost. These things happen."

"You Aryan bastard."

"Just so we understand each other. And if the worst happens and the feds come to investigate, I can always point out that Mark worked with you and hid his DOD file in your file."

"You're a Nazi."

"If you're nice to me and give me your word of honor not to reveal any of this to anyone, I'll rescue your dissertation."

"Graduate students have no honor, but I swear to you on my mother's Bible that I'll be as nice to you as I can and I won't tell anyone about it. What are you going to do with the Pentagon stuff?"

"Erase it."

"I'd like to se it."

"For God's sake, why?"

"I met Mark's father. He's a nice guy and he has suffered a lot because of Mark's suicide. Maybe he should see it. It might help him understand."

"You've got to be kidding. The guy might just march to the Pentagon."

"He won't want to expose his son's crime to them. And, anyway, he's a professor at Berkeley. As a research biologist I bet he gets a lot of money from the federal government, too. He wouldn't want to lose it. Does Bergman know about all this?"

"Mark's father is a professor at Berkeley? I didn't know that."

Did that rate Mark some posthumous respect? "Have you sworn Bergman to secrecy?"

"Dr. Bergman is on federal money."

"We all have federal money. They have guaranteed fifteen thousand dollars of my loans to get me this far. Let me see Mark's stolen file when you get it separated out. And my dissertation. I mean we're all in this together, aren't we? We have to trust each other. How soon do you think you'll have it?"

"As soon as I can without drawing attention from the rest of the staff."

"You're sweating already."

"Pretty girls like you don't sweat?"

"Screw you." She smiled. "And thank you." She kissed him on his fat cheek.

"Any time," he said and wiped his mouth on his sleeve.

When she got to her Mustang she sat for a moment. She felt like crying from relief. She felt the need to tell someone but she hadn't told anyone her research had been lost, except Hans and Mark's father. She drove back to her apartment and brewed some Earl Grey. When Hans returned her data, she wouldn't trust anyone with it again. She would finish her dissertation. If it got accepted and she passed her orals, she would be another goddamned academic looking for a job. Should she tell Michael Horne?

22 LAURIE NEWTON

The early Amtrak train was nearly empty. As it bumped along through the dingy canyons of apartment backsides and into the monotonous suburbs toward Connecticut, Laurie shivered again with the curious sensation she had felt at her brother's funeral. It was the same sensation she had felt as a child when her mother had said that the spirits of the dead were all around them.

"Why aren't they in their graves where they belong?" she said. They were sitting in the upstairs solarium that looked out over the hills of Berkeley.

"Their bodies are in the ground," her mother said, "but their spirits are loosed from their bodies. They are waiting for the day when we shall all be caught up in His glory."

She remembered the odd conviction she had of being outside her body in the blinding sunshine from the east windows. It had been scary, and she put the whole episode from her mind. At the cremation she had suffered the same sensation, a separation from herself, an illusion of something unseen yet present. It was just an emotional reaction, Tom would say. He required concrete evidence for everything. He controlled his life the way he controlled his publishing house, a CPA of living as well as words, scanning every tiny event as though it were a manuscript full of typos, his half glasses perched on the end of his sensitive nose.

Mark had gone off the edge with his lost causes. And then freed himself from them. She turned abruptly to the window so that no one would see her sudden tears. Why did his death affect her so? Her father would go, too. She would lose him. He was a realist like Tom, yet he had always been tolerant of her mother's funny ideas, and of her own conduct.

"Your father's not a believer," her mother said once. "But someday he'll come around. Scientists think everything can be solved logically, but there are things beyond what scientists know."

"Why did you marry him?"

"Because I loved him. He was a graduate assistant in biology and I was a junior taking my postponed science requirement. He helped me. Otherwise I'd never have gotten through the course. I lured him into my clutches."

She remembered being certain he father wouldn't allow himself to fall into clutches unless he chose to.

"Your father came from a small town in Wisconsin, and his family was poor. He got educational benefits because of his service in Korea, and he worked, and got an assistantship. There's nothing wrong with coming from a family without money when you have all the talent he has."

She was surprised at her mother's remark. Had she realized how condescending she sounded?

"My grandfather owned a shipping company in the days when steamships were the only kind of transportation across the ocean. At one time they were among the first families of San Francisco."

"Are we rich?"

Her mother smiled her reassuring smile, crinkling her perfect, pale face. "We have investments and we could manage quite well without your father teaching. Of course, he loves his work and would never quit."

She recalled them talking about the time during the protests on the campus when they had thought about leaving. He was upset that his work might be jeopardized. There were threats about burning the labs. Her father had been opposed both to the war and to the riots. They had considered moving to Canada or England.

Her mother had been dead for ten years, and her father had not changed his ideas. At Mark's funeral she had been shocked at how old he looked. He was planning to retire. She gazed at her reflection in the dirty train window. It was not her face. In her mind she was the face she had been at Smith. She wished she were young and dependent on her father. She was sure of nothing. The small adventures, the rushes of pleasure, the exercise of taste, the chatter with her friends, the house in Connecticut - what did it all come to?

Wasn't she herself, the same person she had always been? If spirits existed, would her mother and Mark be together now, floating around like leaves in the wind? Her mother was corrupted under loam. Mark was about to be strewn to indistinguishable atoms in the ocean. Had he left her his house to connect them again because of the past? His suicide was another kind of abortion. She didn't know why he had done it. She didn't know how she could get rid of him and her past.

The past was sliding away on its own, but staying with her with her against her will. Everything was changing. She was changing. She touched her blouse to check her mole. The Connecticut countryside was gliding by. Grass close to the train was moving in a current of air. She saw a white horse in a field. Birds were hovering over a pond. Were they signs? What did they mean?

What would she do with the rest of her life?

23 *TOM NEWTON*

Only three people got off at Westport, and, of course, Laurie was the last. He worried for a moment she had missed the train. When she did appear, stepping down from the train with her slim, easy grace, he felt the surge of pleasure he always felt when he saw her. He kissed the cheek she offered and stowed her luggage in the trunk of the Lexus. Her perfume stayed with him. As he began to drive, she placed her hand on his knee. Her need for contact.

"How's your father?"

She shook her head. "Mark's death was hard on him. I wish he lived closer. I worry about him."

"He probably feels guilty. Everyone does after a suicide."

"Guilty?" She sounded puzzled and resentful. She took her hand from his knee. "He probably felt weird, like I did."

"Was there a service?"

"We sat for fifteen minutes in a fake chapel, staring at the coffin, and then the coffin went gliding off into the furnace."

"Jesus." He glanced sideways at her face. It was bad enough having a brother kill himself without being put through something like that. She was squinting which meant she was in a state.

"He left his house to me."

"That shack in the mountains?"

"I said I didn't want it. Daddy offered to buy it, so I gave it to him. What would I do with it? Why did Mark do that? Was he trying to tell me something?"

"What will your father do with it? He has the big house in Berkeley. He surely doesn't need it."

"He left his old car to his cleaning woman, his stereo to his girl friend, and his books and prints and papers to Dad."

"His sister, his father, a girl friend and a cleaning woman?"

"He never had anybody else. He was always a loner. Then there was Iraq. We were never close, you know. Which makes it all the weirder that he left me his house. Do we have wills?"

"Of course. Don't you remember signing? With as much involved as we have, we can't let it get eaten up by lawyers. Don't worry about it."

He drove up the long stone road to the house, lifted Laurie's bags from the trunk. Laurie had unlocked the front door with her own key and was waiting for him in the entryway. Before he had a chance to drop her luggage, she grabbed him and held on tightly.

"Tommy," she said into his chest, "I want to have a baby."

He was dumbfounded. "Right now?" he said, trying to be humorous. He sensed her perfume again, the aroma that had always been a part of her.

"Yes! Yes! Let's go to bed." She drew his face down and kissed him passionately on the mouth. She crying and sniffling.
Her tears ran onto his lips. He dropped the bags and they climbed the stairway awkwardly, bumping and hugging.

When they fell apart, she kissed his cheek, his forehead, his nose. Her face was wet with perspiration. And tears again. Were they tears of gratitude that he had acceded to her wish, or was it anguish still at her brother's death? She had fallen asleep. She always did, almost at once. Even with the sun streaming in.

He extricated himself from her arms and padded into the sitting room. Laurie was simple in some ways, but he loved her more than he could describe. His love was physical and ethereal at the same time. Treetops were swaying in the wind and birds were making their usual noises. In the mornings and in the evenings the sound of birds was sometimes overwhelming. Sunlight flickered in patterns through the leaves and curtains on the wood floor where he stood, naked and aware of his breathing. This, too, was almost ethereal. He loved it here. He loved Laurie and his work. He didn't want to think of suicide and death. There was no use in that. It was simply one generation and another like the seasons. The sun coming up and going down.

Laurie called to him. She was not asleep after all. He entered the bedroom again and sat beside her on the bed. Without looking at him, she found his hand and twined her fingers around his and stared at the ceiling. Strands of her long, black hair fell loose across her forehead, her face shiny in the bright sunlight. Her naked body stirred him toward desire again.

"Why did Mark leave his house to me?"

"Maybe he had no one else to leave it to." It was still on her mind. If he knew her, the house would become an obsession.

She tightened her grip on his hand. "When I was little, my mother told me that the spirits of the dead were all around us. She could sense them. And I had this eerie sensation at Mark's funeral that he was really there."

She was talking in a monotonous voice toward the ceiling. She sighed and turned to him. "I know you don't believe in things like that." She looked at him like a child asking a parent to understand. She turned her eyes away again and loosened her hand. She closed her eyes and was silent for a moment, then she spoke in a low voice toward the luminous windows:

"Everything seems strange to me. Life is strange. Making life is strange. What a funny way to make a life, fitting our bodies together. Dying is strange. Why should we die? If our bodies die, what about the rest of us, our real self, whatever you want to call it, what happens to that? It's all crazy."

24 *JIMMY HORNE*

He did not look forward to going home to his condominium.

When they separated, Marie had demanded the house in Walnut Creek, the furniture, the horses, as well as half their accumulated estate. He had to start at scratch to furnish his new place, and discovered that not only did he not have the heart, he didn't have any ideas. The house he grew up in Berkeley had been furnished in an eclectic style with heirlooms and things his mother had chosen, all appropriate but none belonging anywhere else.

He didn't want some professional decorator to fill his condo with the latest fluff. He thought of asking the woman who decorated his office to give him some suggestions, but never got around to asking her. The place retained the appearance of being about to redone or moved out of.

And there was no one waiting or him when he did get home.

Sometimes the women he brought home offered to decorate for him. He did not wish to be obligated to anyone. He ate out mostly, except for breakfast, and that was a nuisance because the condo was not near a good restaurant. He sat in his car in the underground parking garage, facing the number that corresponded to the number of his condo and breathed deeply. He picked up his briefcase and went to the elevator. Linda was curled up on the floor in front of his door.

He felt a jolt of apprehension.

"Linda?"

She jumped up. "Daddy," she called. She plunged into his arms and burst into tears. He had just seen her in the Spring play. What could have happened? He managed to unlock the door and get them inside.

"Would you like a drink?"

She nodded. He dropped his briefcase and sat her gently on the sofa and went to the bar. He fixed two Scotches with ice from the ice maker.

Linda accepted the glass with both hands, drank, gulped and coughed. She handed the glass back to him.

"Can you talk now? Is there something wrong at school?"

She hiccupped and sighed. He gave her a handkerchief from his lapel pocket. She wiped her eyes and blew her nose.

"I've got herpes."

"How do you know?"

"The doctor told me."

"Which doctor?"

"Does it matter? It was the school doctor."

She was right. He was too much the lawyer. There were no loopholes with herpes.

"Herpes is not the end of the world."

"It *is* the end of the world."

"What exactly did the doctor say?"

"That I have herpes. That there is no cure for herpes. That I should be careful about giving it to someone else by sexual contact. That I should be careful about having a baby. That herpes is highly contagious when the symptoms are showing, and even when they're not, it can be contagious. That potential sexual partners should be warned so that they can take protective measures."

"They have drugs to help."

"To relieve symptoms and reduce outbreaks."

"There are millions of people who have herpes. They manage to live their lives. You have to adjust to it, that's all."

"What do I do? Tell every guy I meet that I have herpes?"

"Not unless you intend to sleep with them."

"That's mean."

"Linda, it really isn't the end of the world. There are far worse things. When ugly things happen we have to learn to go on. You are young and bright and attractive. You have a problem that will require some changes, but you have a whole life ahead of you."

"I want to die."

"Because you've got blisters in your crotch?"

"That was cheap and cruel," she shouted. "You're making fun of me."

"I'm sorry. I know it's upsetting. So get angry. But don't give up. It's not AIDS, which really is serious. Isn't it about time for spring break? You could come here and stay for the break, or for however long you wish. Have you told your mother?"

"You know how she would react. I can't tell her."

"We'll drive to the campus in the morning to get your things. You can cut the classes you have before the break."

She snuggled into his arms again, as she had when she was six. It wasn't fair. He wanted to kill the guy who had given it to her.

"I have a friend at the medical school. I'm sure he can get all the latest information. We'll do what we can now, and keep up with whatever is happening. I have a trial coming up, but I'll take off all the time I can. We'll go riding and sailing like we used to. Do plays and concerts, whatever you appeals to you."

She turned weepy again. Now what had he said?

"What about your private life?"

Her mother had been talking to her.

"No woman friend is as important to me as my daughter. Now, how about some supper? We can go out, or I have some frozen pizza. I have eggs, bacon, rye bread, kosher dills pepperoncini, Wisconsin cheddar, and chocolate ice cream."

"Let's stay in."

"I'll see what I can whip up." He got up, removed his jacket, and went into the kitchen. The florescent flickered on. Linda followed. "How about an omelet?" He washed his hands, got out a bowl, eggs, cheese, and began chopping an onion. Linda found plates, wine glasses, silver, and a bottle of Pinot Grigio and set up the eating bar. He turned on the kitchen stereo. Vivaldi. Linda had once taken cello lessons. He steered the conversation to her college courses. She was doing well. She liked her courses in the humanities, especially French. Her science courses were hard. She might major in drama.

Finally, she yawned. He showed her the spare bedroom, with its spare furnishings, where to find towels in the guest bathroom. He gave her a goodnight hug.

He went to his room, hung up his jacket, went to the bath to wash his face. Why did these things happen? Marie would say everything evil was the result of sin. His father would say that viruses are just another form of life. When they find a host home, they lodge there and multiply. What did that do for any meaning for human beings? In the midst of beauty there was ugliness, stupidity, disease. Mark had been unable to live in a world he thought unjust from the beginning. But the world was not unjust; it was indifferent. If you rejected the world, there was nothing. The world was what there was. People were what they were. You had to accommodate.

25 *LEAH STEIN*

When she reached the turnoff, her heart was pounding. She sat at the row of mailboxes, breathing deeply. She was mad to think of coming up here. She retrieved the mail that had accumulated in Mark's box. Bills, a computer magazine, junk. She climbed the dirt road in first gear and pulled up to the front door.

Orin had returned to Chicago. He had put the La Jolla house on the market. It would bring more than a million dollars in the current market. She had given up her condo and put her furniture in storage when she moved in with Lydia. Could she find a place to live she could afford? Mark had complained about his long commute from Alpine, but he had refused to consider moving back to the city. Dr. Horne surely had no use for the house. He had obviously accepted it from Laurie for emotional reasons.

When she approached the door she saw that it was open. The frame had been splintered. She stepped back. There was no car in the yard other than her own. There would surely be no one in the house. Unless someone remained behind. Or were they on foot? She peered through the door into the dark interior, ready to spring back and run for her car. Anyone in the house would have heard her drive up. She stepped in carefully. The house was a wreck, furniture turned over, books, lamps and pictures scattered across the floor.

Who could have done such a thing? Not José and Lupe. Why?

Was it mere vandalism? What could they imagine they could find behind books, under lamps or chairs. Jimmy had been right to insist she take the stereo at once. The computer was gone, the television. She looked into the kitchen. The refrigerator was gone. They must have had a truck. In the bedroom she found clothes strewn over the floor. The digital clock radio was gone.

She wanted to cry. She needed a drink.

Without thinking, she began to pick up Mark's clothes and hang them in the closet. She returned to the living room and picked up pieces of furniture, righted chairs. She gathered books and placed them on shelves. She was caught up in bringing the house to order. The microwave oven was gone. She rescued pans and items of canned food, boxes of cereal. They had not taken food or clothes. What they had stolen were items they could quickly sell. Had they made the mess or the pleasure of it? Or was it an act of anger? Druggies needing money to buy drugs? She secured a trash bag and gathered broken pieces of dishes and glasses and vitamin capsules.

As she collected things, she found herself on her knees in front of the chair where Mark had sat, at the edge of the dark stain. She caught her breath to stop the unexpected sob that rose in her throat. She took the trash bag to the kitchen and opened the garage door to put the bag in the container where Mark had kept his trash. She had to push the cabinet aside. Its contents had been scattered. The Volvo was gone.

In the kitchen again, she took a bucket from under the sink and filled it with hot water. There was hot water, so the heater was on. They hadn't cut off the utilities yet. She would pay the bills and send Dr. Horne any personal mail. She dumped soap in the bucket, found a sponge along the sink and went into the living room. She began to scrub. The chair, the rug, trying not to think of bits of brain and bone and skin and blood. She washed the pieces of Mark's body away. Her uncle Moshe had been the first dead man she had seen. Her mother and her aunts had washed the body. They said it was the custom in the old country for the women to prepare the body for burial. She poured the water down the sink and rinsed the bucket. The women. It was only through the women that the blood

119

line continued.

Mark was not of her blood, but she had shared with him her angers against war and government, politicians, bureaucrats, establishments. And they had shared their love for art, music, movies, jazz. They had gone to lectures, movies, museums, concerts together. They had been kin in their pleasures and estrangements. She hadn't known about the shed and the illegals. Had he thought that because she worked for the county welfare department she would not approve? Were illegals still using the shed on their inland route to *El Norte*?

She went out the back door and gazed over the edge of the slope. It was still there. There was no sign of life. She descended the circular path and peeked into the shed. Empty. Light fell on the mattress. The dark stains of birth.

She returned to the house out of breath, filled the bucket with hot water again, added soap, and made her way down to the shed. Scrubbed, threw the soapy water into the canyon. Climbed again, collected cans of food, filled empty water bottles, put them in a trash bag and dragged them down the path, lined the cans and bottles along the floor. What had happened to Lupe and José? She let the door open to the air. Would Mark trust her now?

She was out of her mind to think of trying to justify herself to a dead man. Mark had been a friend. Lydia had been a friend. Now she was without either, as abandoned and homeless in her psyche as the Mexican illegals. She climbed the path back to the house.

She had humiliated herself with Orin, subject to needs that were caught in some crooked corner of herself. She would expurgate Orin. Appease Mark. She would put out food and water for the illegals as they crossed the borders of despair to this fucked-up promised land. She would live with deliberation her separate life, a misfit dealing with misfits, accepting her separateness in a loco pact with a corrupt society. And exorcise her father.

She sat in Mark's chair, still damp from scrubbing. She was a loony. But this would be her life. With Mark. With Lydia. She would perform her work. Come home to Mark's house, bring back the stereo and listen to blues. Watch the mountain shadows list eastward from the scuttling sun. Peace. She wanted to be at peace with herself.

26 *MICHAEL HORNE*

As he entered his study, the phone rang. He was damp from running on the seawall. The jolts to his bones, and especially to his cranium, seemed to shake loose one thought and cause the eruption of another. Or maybe he was just weary of pondering, in his persistent way, the contradictions of scientific ethics.

It was Leah. It hadn't been that long since she had called with her desperate news about Mark. She was at Mark's house, having gone out to collect his mail and check on Lupe and José. The Mexicans had departed, but the house had been looted. The computer, television, refrigerator, microwave, and Volvo had all been stolen. The front door had been forced. Should she inform the police? And would he rent the house to her, or sell it to her? It was better to have it occupied. Her friend had died and she needed to find an new place to live.

He was dismayed. He told her he would be happy to rent the house to her, agreeing that it was better to have someone in it. He'd have to think about selling it. He would have to check with Jimmy since Jimmy was the executor. Did she have a refrigerator? He thought rental houses provided stoves and refrigerators. The stove was still there. She had her own refrigerator, presently in storage.

121

He called Jimmy's office to discover that Jimmy was taking the week off. He dialed his home number and Linda answered.

"Linda? It's Michael, your grandfather."

"Grandpa?"

"What a surprise. You're at your father's place? I thought you were in school."

"It's spring break. I'm spending one week with Dad and one with Mom." She sounded very young and shaky.

"Are you okay?"

"I'm fine, more or less. But I'm ready for a vacation. How are you?"

"All right. Thinking hard and writing a paper."

"Dad says you're writing a paper on bio-ethics or something like that."

"Something like that."

"Do they need bio-ethics in Texas?"

"More than any place except California."

She laughed.

"Actually, the people here are quite nice. And helpful. And opinionated. As your father can tell you, I'm not opinionated at all."

"You sound just the same, even in Texas. I'm sorry about Uncle Mark. I didn't know him very well. Daddy said I shouldn't attend the funeral." She sounded on the verge of tears.

Though she hadn't known Mark, her emotional state appeared suddenly to have connected. He didn't know Linda the way he knew Laurie and had known Janice, but he thought he had an ear for tone. Something was wrong, and it was not something she did wished to talk about.

"I understand. Is your father there?"

When Jimmy came on, he asked about Linda and got the same response. They weren't talking. This was his place again: separated from their lives as though he were a distant relative.

Jimmy advised that Leah's discovery should be reported to the police, especially since the Volvo was specifically mentioned in the will and would have to be accounted for. The cleaning woman also deserved an explanation since she may have known that Mark had left her the car. As executor, he would draw up a lease for

Leah. How much rent did he intend to charge?

Michael said he would find out what such a house might rent for in Alpine. He would send money to Leah and ask her to buy the cleaning woman a car equivalent to, or better, to the old Volvo. Jimmy said that was not required, but he could do that if he so desired.

Michael relayed Jimmy's agreement to rent the house to Leah at a rate she believed appropriate, and explained his wish that she purchase a car for the cleaning woman to replace the stolen Volvo, if she would be so kind. He would send a check for whatever amount of money might be required. He showered away the sweat from his running, donned a pair of cotton shorts, and lowered himself stiffly into his desk chair. The air conditioner was working at full power. It was time to take a careful look at what he had come to so far. The assumptions on which he would base his extended essay would, no doubt, be controversial to most potential readers.

As Richard Dawkins had rightly complained, philosophy and the humanities were taught as if Darwin had never existed. How could the basic issues of philosophy, including ethics, even be raised without recognizing that we were creatures subject to the ineluctable drive to survive and replicate? Did philosophy exist apart from biological nature, the hypothalamus, the limbic system?

Morality was not inherent in nature, but rather consisted historically of the "mores" of tribes. Yet survival and reproduction were the underlying bases for tribal customs - enmeshed in myths and the "revelations" of charismatic leaders.

At the heart of every culture lay a kind of primitive science, explanations of origins and nature. Rigidified, these explanations, in the hands of priests and politicians, became the foundation of power.

The fundamental character of tribal cultures that had its basis in myth continued today. "Ethics" for the population derived from our "culture," not from what we knew of our biology and evolution. We had not evolved for some external "purpose". The "purpose" of every cell in us was to survive and replicate. It was that which we obeyed - without consciously willing to. Not our fathers, or a Big Father (who complained historically - and still did, if you still took it all seriously, through His presumptuous, self-appointed spokespersons - about our disobedience to paternal power).

That being the case, we were obliged to understand our underlying natures; and our ethical problem became how best, without coercion, to enhance our survival as individuals, as societies, as the human race. At minimum, that meant not harming each other, our own or other societies, or the human race, for the sake of religion, or political ideologies, or sheer shortsighted greed. We had to continue to discover our nature, and take our awareness of it into account when we made judgments or attempted to impose rules on human conduct.

He levered himself from his chair and made for the kitchen, uncapped a cold Hougaese Das.

Of course the progress of science got stalled from time to time in its own historical rigidities, the paradigm of the moment, before someone broke through again. Yet the impulse toward discovery was as much a part of the basic nature of evolutionary humans as both mutation and the conservative replication of DNA. The core of human curiosity and exploration could never be quashed. As Galileo said, under his breath: *eppur si mouve.*

His quarrel was not with practicing medical ethicists who dealt with real people, laden with their religions, scruples and emotions as they faced medical decisions. Henry O'Leary's book, *Deciding to Die*, was, as he had told Henry, a sensible, practical guide. His quarrel was with theologians and ethicists who, being ignorant of, or ignoring, science, aspired to control it. Jay Gould had remarked that "Much of the history of science has been a withdrawal of theology from these disciplines."

But that same Jay Gould had approvingly cited the Supreme Court decision of 1987 which held that science and religion operated in equally legitimate areas. The mechanisms and phenomena of nature were allotted to the scientists and the bases for ethical decisions to theologians and humanists. The trouble with that separatist position was that the sides could no more be separate but equal than blacks and whites.

And, in any case, the religionists insisted on telling scientists what they could not do, and the scientists kept uncovering facts about nature that undermined the assumptions of the religionists. Philosophers were game players; they were required only to be follow the rules. And humanists, of course, cared more for history and lore than scientific knowledge.

The phone again.

"It's Vanessa. Remember me?"

"Very well. Did you ever find your computer file?"

"Yes, thank heavens."

"Terrific."

"I need to talk to you."

"Go ahead."

"In person. I know it sounds odd, but I have some confidential information about Mark."

"Too confidential for phone or email?"

"So I've been told. I agreed I wouldn't show you the material I have, except in person. Or maybe you'd just as soon not go through all that again."

"I'd like to see, or hear what you have. Shall I fly out there, or can you come here?"

"I can go there, if you like. I don't have money for airfare."

"Southwest is the outfit I used when I went to San Diego. I'll have my agent make arrangements with you at your convenience. I'll be here at least another month. He'll call you and then let me know the arrangements. There is a van from Hobby, the nearest airport to Galveston and where Southwest will bring you. You can give my address to the driver and he'll being you directly to the house. You can stay with me, if you don't mind. I have a whole house to myself."

"You're very efficient."

"Only when I need to be. I appreciate your willingness to do this, and I look forward to seeing you again. What is your number there?"

She gave him her number and he gave her his address. He called his travel agent.

Would learning more about Mark's death ease the pain of it?

An image of a sterile, white church rose in his mind: the coffin on its stand, replacing the communion table, and, surmounting it, the pulpit where the preacher in a mixture of King James' English and bad American grammar, commended his father to heaven. The quavering voices of the congregation filled his ears again. At the back of the platform in an arched alcove was the tank into which at the age of seven he had been more or less forcibly dunked. He had emerged, his clothes soaked and heavy on him, gasping for breath, saved.

The memories of his father's funeral and his own salvation by drowning flickered in his head like an anthropologist's amateur movie of primitive rites. They were part of him, irradicable.

The phone rang into his memories.

"Michael? Lou Cutter. How are you doing?"

"Okay, I think."

"We're having some people over this afternoon about five or so, people you know, and Therese and I were wondering whether you'd join us."

"I'd be happy to."

"We're pleased."

He pushed his computer back, loosing a cataract of books and scribbled notes to the floor. If he did complete a paper that contained his honest views, would it be so much against the grain, so contrary to the opinions of the keepers of the public morals, that he would be regarded as a crank?

His travel agent rang. Vanessa would be arriving the following afternoon. He was surprised at how quickly she had decided to come, and surprised to find himself cheered by the prospect of her coming.

He collected his papers from the floor and piled them on his table in an order that would make them easier to follow.

His inner clock nudged him. He saw that it was five. He donned slacks and a Guayaberra shirt and sandals and headed for the Cutters. The Cutter house, beyond the protection of the seawall, was perched on stilts to stay above the tidal floods that accompanied storms and hurricanes.

Therese greeted him with a hug. "We glad you could come. We were terribly sorry to hear about your son." Therese was thin as crepe and wore skin-tight jeans that revealed there was nothing to reveal.

Lou shook his hand. Lou was a shortened version of Magnum P.I. The Cutters had two sons and three dogs. Lou was an ethicist and Therese was an artist. They were careless housekeepers and genial hosts. They had welcomed him warmly when he first arrived, and Lou had helped him find his way around the university.

Several of the guests spoke in condolence. He took his drink to the deck where it was almost tolerable in the evening breeze off the Gulf. There were mosquitoes. Kippy Krammer took his arm.

"I wanted to thank you personally for your generous donation to the Guild. We have received almost enough to survive another year."

"I believe in survival," he said, smiling. "And I liked your latest exhibition, especially Therese Cutter's photographs. Some talented people here."

"We like to think so." She patted stray hair into place. "Galveston doesn't have the resources, or the audience, Houston has. Even our humanists here are indifferent to the local artists."

"It must not be easy."

As Kippy released one arm, Natalia touched the other. "One of my students attended the lecture where the Nobelist speaker claimed that the soul was located between the synapses. She was impressed by your comments."

He laughed. "I suppose it was impolite of me to take on a Nobelist. As a physiologist, Eccles had to locate the soul somewhere, I suppose. Dualism is a western bias that has powerful devotees. Plato. The Christians. Descartes thought the soul was in the pineal gland. I favor the liver myself."

Natalia regarded him skeptically. "I gather you don't believe in altruism. Wasn't that his topic?"

"I think so. Well, as he said, altruism pays off. That's because it isn't altruism. It's an inherent survival trait."

"The mosquitoes are getting to me," she said, and took off.

"Me too," he said to the breeze.

He encountered Henry O'Leary at the bar. "Have you heard from the publisher?"

"Not yet," Henry said. "My editor recommended it to the publisher. No okay from the publisher yet. How's your paper?"

"I'm still working on it."

"I know you're a biologist," Henry said. "And you've done work on genes and DNA. Doesn't it worry you that we are intervening in nature with genetic engineering and the like?"

"Doctors in your hospitals intervene in nature all the time. Isn't that the heart of medicine? And if disease is natural, aren't doctors and drugs a part of nature? Genetic engineering has been going on for a long time, otherwise we wouldn't have enough food. That's why we have dogs for pets, not wolves. But you're raising a bigger question. You can't stop knowledge, including the knowledge of genes and DNA. And you shouldn't try to stop it because some it might be misused. Should we have stopped the development of airplanes because terrorists might use them as weapons? There will always be people who will misuse and abuse whatever we invent or learn. We should stop the terrorists, not science.

"And when you say 'intervention' you're assuming that Somebody Up There set us on a course that we can intervene in. The point is there is no outside from which to intervene. Everything *is* nature, including genes, debris from space, ice ages, mutations, humans and their brains and their biological knowledge."

He saw that all eyes were on him. "Sorry," he said. "I tend to lecture, especially on my favorite subjects."

"Stuff about science is all in the mind, anyway," Natalie said her perch on a bar stool.

"Maybe you're right. But if you're of a mind to fly from the roof, you may run into Isaac Newton."

There was laughter. A few more drinks Natalie would be ready to aviate. Children's voice and gunfire sounded from the TV in the recreation room.

"Okay, so everything is nature," Henry said. "You still haven't said who within all this nature should make decisions, or on what basis." He pointed to the bar. "More Scotch?"

"Those who have knowledge, including scientific knowledge, not those who would base them on theology or politics. Two's my limit."

"Don't you think the society which will be affected by decisions of that sort ought to have a say? What about the traditions of that society? What about decisions rooted in history?"

"If your history incorporates human biology and evolutionary science. As any neurologist can tell you, when things happen to our physical selves, including our brains, whether as a result of outside events, or aroused by chemicals or electrical events within, things happen to our thinking and our judgments. Shouldn't we take them into account?"

"I'm not sure how you would, or that it's relevant."

Maybe Henry was right. How would you take it all into account? Knowledge of the irresistible instincts that underlay human conduct were not things that most humans possessed, or wanted to possess. With a few apologetic remarks, and with thanks to the Cutters for their hospitality, he took his leave. They were good people. They didn't have to agree with him.

Without conscious intention, he drove to the west end of the island, and over sand and grass to the rim of a Gulf that reached to the Caribbean where the Caymans banked drug money for the dealers, to Columbia and its drug farms, to Cuba and its out-of-date dictator, to the Antilles where hurricanes bred. In the water, and in the sand under his feet, and in the systems of his body were billions of life forms, unique and beautiful, reproducing, dying. To what end finally? Decimation, death, the end of every consciousness? Was it a question that had no answer and thus no meaning? And, in all the trivia of drugs and dictators and cocktail parties and pickup trucks and jelly fish and discarded plastic and sexually abusive priests and corrupt politicians and Islamic terrorists, did it matter?

27 VANESSA PARSONS

When she followed the driver from the baggage claim area toward the parking garage where the van was waiting, she was struck by a blast of hot air that made her gasp.

"Jesus. Is it always like this?"

The driver laughed. "Only six months a year."

Watching the landscape go by, she was dismayed. It was like the worst of Los Angeles. A fungus of car dealers, gas stations, shopping malls, billboards, fast food joints, scrub trees. Then little houses on stilts in swamps. Why would Michael Horne leave the green hills of Berkeley for an island in a swamp?

The van pulled up on a street of scrawny trees in front of a two story yellow Victorian house with white gingerbread trim. Her distress at the environment began to ease, but her anxiety about how Michael might react to the information he brought about his son began to rise. As she descended from the van and approached the house, Michael appeared in the door in unpressed cords and a white polo shirt. His bronzed face was smiling. He reached for her bag and leaned his back against the door to hold it open.

"Quickly, out of the heat," he said. Her bag in his left hand, he closed the door and extended his right to shake hers.

"I appreciate your coming. Let me show you right away where you'll be." He led the way up the stairs. He pointed to the rear of the house into a small room that looked into the tops of trees. Most of the room was occupied by a four poster bed.

"The bath next door is all yours. I live in the front and have my own bath. You can freshen up if you wish. I'm in the downstairs study which is to your left as you come down."

"Thanks for your hospitality," she said. "I'll being Mark's stuff with me when I come down."

"No hurry."

As she descended the stair, her apprehension increased. How would he react? She found him his study, his back to her, in a swivel chair, leaning over a desk covered with papers. The Miró print she had seen in Alpine rested at an angle against the wall. Music came from a portable stereo on the floor beside him.

He turned suddenly. "Sorry, I didn't hear you." He stood. Since when had a professor stood for her? He pointed to a chair at the side of the desk.

"We can talk here if you like. Would you like a beer, or some iced tea?"

"Iced tea, if you don't have to brew it."

"I put the kettle on when I came back down stairs. The water should be hot. I'll get it for you." He started for the kitchen.

"May I come with you?"

"Just don't look too closely at my kitchen. I have a cleaning woman who comes once a week to clean and straighten up properly."

The kitchen was messy but not dirty. Upside down pans were drying in the sink strainer. Newspapers were piled on the table where he obviously had his solitary meals.

He worked deftly, pouring hot water into a glass with a tea bag in it, dipping the bag until it was the right color, and added ice cubes. "Lemon? Sugar?"

"Lemon."

His hands were thickened as though he had worked with them all his life. His hair was dense and brown, tinged with gray, the edges unkempt. He found a lemon, sliced it carefully, handed her the glass. He secured a beer from the refrigerator, and pointed her toward the study.

"I'm surprised you drink beer. It looks foreign."

He laughed as he uncapped the bottle. "I should drink Scotch and soda, smoke a pipe and love Irish setters?"

She laughed. "I guess beer didn't fit my image of you."

"I'm just a small town boy from Wisconsin, the beer-loving state. Actually the beer is Hougaerdse Das, from Belgium. It's spiced with coriander and orange peel. I like to experiment with beers."

She sipped her tea and he drank with seeming appreciation and, raised his eyebrows expectantly.

She opened the folder she had brought with her. "These are printouts of the data Mark hid in the computer by mixing them with other files. You remember my dissertation file was lost? It was found by Dr. Bergman, a biologist who does cancer research."

"Saul Bergman?"

"Yes. Do you know him?"

"Saul did graduate work with me at Berkeley. I recommended him to UCSD. How did he find your file?"

"What he found was that an old file of his was messed up. As it turned out, the mess was created by Mark by interleaving Bergman's file with my file and data Mark had extracted from Pentagon files. Since Bergman had not been using this particular file, Mark could access all three files by accessing Bergman's file.

"When Bergman tried to review his old file, he found it in chaos and went to Hans Dieter who was Mark's assistant and is now acting director of academic computing. Hans discovered the triple layering, and figured out that what Mark was doing was hiding the material he had hacked from the Pentagon." She took a deep breath.

"What he was finally able to sort out was that Mark had hacked data from Pentagon about an attack by American soldiers on unarmed Iraqi civilians. Mark's unit had been attacked hours before the event by a group of what they assumed were former Iraqi soldiers now in civilian clothes. The unit searched for their attackers and came across a group of civilians who, as it turned out, were not their attackers."

She handed the printout to Michael who had been listening intently. He set his beer bottle down carefully on some reprints and accepted the printouts.

"Apparently a confidential investigation was made and Mark got hold of the report. He added some comments of his in pen at the end."

Michael started to read. She wondered whether she should stay or leave. He might especially want to be alone when he read the comments Mark had added.

"Would you like to be by yourself? I can go upstairs."

"No. That's all right. Stay."

He was reading quickly. The reports were dry and factual, except that they referred to a possible atrocity committed by a unit of the United States Army.

The question was whether the civilians were killed knowingly or whether the Americans made a mistake. Mark had been wounded in the earlier attack on his unit and was a participant in the killing of the civilians. A copy of his individual record contained the notation that he been awarded the Silver Star and a Purple Heart.

When Michael came to the third page, she looked away. It wouldn't be proper for her to watch him when he read Mark's final words. He finished reading. She kept her gaze out the window through gauzy curtains, sipped her tea.

We knew. Because of my wound, I was unable to fire, but I was there. I wanted to kill them. I came back like a ghost to live out my death. Let me lie with those I murdered, and who murdered me. Forgive me, Mother."

She heard a drawer open. Michael was blowing his nose. "It's okay," he said hoarsely. "I'm glad you brought this to me." His face was half turned. He picked up his bottle without drinking.

"Hans insisted this material should not be sent through the mails or phoned," she said, "because it was taken illegally from the Department of Defense files. If they found out that Mark had hacked into their files, Hans thought they might take action against UCSD, and cut off research funds."

Michael shook his head, wiped his eyes on a tissue, stared at the wall. He breathed deeply and said: "Remember the folder I took from Mark's cabinet in Alpine?"

"I remember."

He rubbed his forehead as though to erase his emotions. "It

was a copy of a section of my journal. I've kept a journal since high school. My English teacher got me started. She said we should talk to ourselves. Anyway, the section of my journal that Mark copied was about the death of a friend, Mark's godfather. Noah was dying of cancer. The excerpt is about my helping him to die. I don't know how he got hold of my journal, or how he interpreted what I did."

"It must have been important to him."

He looked beyond her, silent again for a moment. "It was all so long ago. He left his papers to me in his will. He wanted me to know that he knew. He must been aware that Saul Bergman had been a student of mine, and he used Bergman's research to hide this material. He wanted to make a point. He wanted to tie me into this terrible event, to make me responsible for his death. For his mother's death. For Noah's death. For the government's deceit. It's happened before. Korea, Viet Nam. And now Iraq. We're all guilty. And the guilt goes back a long way." There was a tremor in the hand that spanned his eyes. "He couldn't let it go."

He was clearly deeply pained by the news she brought, and linked it to the other things he had been through with Mark beyond it. She felt awkward. "Maybe he needed to unload everything on you as the most important person in his life. He must have wanted your understanding." She paused. "Sorry, I should be intruding with my opinions."

"You're very perceptive. And perhaps you're right. I'm glad you came. It's better to know, even when it hurts." He took another shaky breath. His effort not to burden her with his feelings made his voice tight. "Anyhow it's good to have a budding academic to talk with."

"I'm a way from being a full-fledged academic," she said softly.

"But with your dissertation recovered, you're on the way."

"I hope."

"Tell me again what your thesis is about. Our first discussion about it was rather brief, as I recall."

"I have a knack for being brief, for reducing big topics to instant coffee. And I'm not sure how to state my thesis in any case. I'll say it's about the conflict between the individual protagonist and the society around him. It's about alienation and continuity."

"You think that conflict is inherent in our culture?"

"I don't know about our culture. But I think it's a pattern in serious novels. What are *you* working on? You must have something pretty important on your menu to come to this place."

Michael smiled. "Galveston is not as bad as it looks at first glance. I'm here because there is a well-known institute here. Their field is medical humanities. Some of them focus on medical ethics. My interest is in the basis for ethics in science. I thought they might steer me to sources and offer criticism of my notions about it.

"What am I working on? Something like what you are working on. Only instead of alienation and continuity, I call it mutation and conservation. We could compare notes. In a novel the alienated (I would say mutated) hero, after all his struggles and adventures, uses his difference, call it his new-found self-knowledge, if you prefer, to understand himself and to protect his continuity, his integration into his environment. Of course, there are lots of dead ends - for heroes as well as for species. Am I stretching things?"

"Sounds good to me. Maybe *you* should write my dissertation."

He laughed. His mood had eased.

"Isn't that the kind of biology you do all the time?" she said. "Where do you get ethics out of the theory of evolution? Isn't ethics supposed to be a philosophical or religious affair? What's ethical behavior for an evolutionist?"

"Aha. For me, at least, ethical behavior means acquiring knowledge and passing it on without restraint; seeing knowledge as an end in itself, and, at the same time, using it to assure our survival as human beings on our solitary planet; trying to stop the destruction of our habitat because of ignorance, or greed, or blind political ideology."

"That's a pretty heavy charge."

"I'm becoming didactic." He leaned back in his chair. "I might go on lecturing forever, except that my ability to lecture and yours to listen depends on more practical things, like food. Galveston has some surprisingly good places to eat. If you like Italian, Luigi has the best in town."

"Shall I wear a dress?"

"Luigi doesn't mind what you wear."

She showered, washed her hair and blew it dry, put on her one conventional dress, and applied her usual small amount of lipstick.

Luigi's restaurant had once been a bank, when Galveston had once been the major seaport and the biggest city in Texas, Michael said. They sat in an area that had been a vault. Its walls now were lined with racks in which Luigi stored his bottles of wine.

In his gray slacks and gray tweed jacket, Michael looked distinguished, in an academic way. She aspired to be like him, she thought, amused. He ordered wine for her and a single malt Scotch for himself. He smiled when he ordered it. He quizzed her about herself. She found herself telling him about the ghetto where she grew up, her father's abandonment, her mother's crucial encouragement, her obsessive drive to educate herself. He reacted with obvious admiration.

In turn, she asked him about his own background, and he told her about Wisconsin and his parents, about his wife, Janice, and their children (she reminded him she had met them all), about his research in evolutionary biology.

"I keep wanting to believe there is some kind of design to it all, some kind of God. A divine conscience in people that makes us care about each other and treat each other fairly," she said.

"You care for each other in your family, don't you?"

"Except for my father. He doesn't care about anybody but himself."

"And you came all the way out here to bring me Mark's stuff. Why did you do that?"

"I don't know. In fact I thought Mark was trying to do me in, and I was mad at him. I think now he was hurt and angry, maybe a little out of his mind to begin with, or because of the things that happened to him. He used me, I think. I don't believe now that he meant to hurt me. I got to know you out in Alpine, and I liked you, and I thought you deserved to know. Why did you help the Mexicans?"

"So you don't do things for your own immediate benefit."

"I don't know. Maybe everything I do is for my own self-interest. You think it's altruism when we do things for other people?"

"No. There is no such thing as altruism. When you do things for other people it really is in your own interest."

"You've lost me. Anyway, do you really think you can persuade sold-out politicians, religious nuts, racial fanatics, and Harvard MBAs to cooperate and do what they ought so that we can all to survive? They can't see beyond their mustaches."

Michael smiled at her. "I'm trying to quarry granite with a razor."

"I like that," she said. He likes me, she thought. She smiled back at him.

"Cardinal Newman. He said using reason and knowledge against passion and pride was like quarrying granite with a razor or mooring a vessel with a silk thread."

The food was good. Luigi himself came to their table to greet Michael. Michael introduced him to her. He sang a piece of Rigoletto for her in a powerful operatic tenor to the applause of the house.

On the way back to Michael's house, he drove along the seawall so that she could observe the Gulf and the lights coruscating in the waves. Once at the house, they sat in the study and talked about books. He had read far beyond her own reading. She expressed surprise. "You've read more than Darwin's *Voyage of the Beagle,*" she said.

He laughed. And then, catching her yawning, he suggested it might be the hour for her to go to bed. She got up, hesitated, then kissed him on the cheek and thanked him for dinner. He said he would stay up for a little longer, but that in the morning it was his habit to run along the seawall. If she would like to join him, he would be happy to have her run with him. Wake me, if I'm not up already, she said.

The four poster was higher off the ground than she had ever slept. Her bed in San Diego was a mattress on the floor. She rehearsed her day, as was her wont, thinking of Michael reading the printouts about Iraq, and the epitaph Mark had written for himself.

She hadn't told him the whole story. Hans had called her, practically screaming, to say that after he had run out her thesis, Dr. Bergman's research and the stuff on Iraq, the computer erased them. Then other files began to disappear. Mark had inserted a virus. Did she realize what that would mean? All the research files were in peril. And his friend at UCLA told him he had heard there was a virus in the some of the Pentagon files. If Mark did it, would they trace it back here?

She told him she knew nothing about it. He was frantic. He had a trouble shooter looking. He told her not to say anything about it to anyone. He would find out if she did.

She felt sorry for Hans. If a catastrophe occurred on his watch, his chances of getting Mark's job would be nil. She felt sorry for the researchers who might lose their files. She had her file. She could finish her dissertation. There was nothing she could do for the others. Why had Mark done it? James Joyce might have said that Mark couldn't wake up from the nightmare of his history. Was he incorporating everyone into his own?

She couldn't tell Michael. He had suffered enough with the suicide and the Pentagon printout. And Hans had warned her. Was it all a cry to his father for pity? She had wanted her own father to love and care for her. Was he his own victim? She fell asleep, distressed for gentle Michael, for her own traitorous, lost father.

28 *MICHAEL HORNE*

They drove to the west end of the island and jogged toward the rising sun, dodging seaweed and trash washed ashore from passing freighters and oil rigs, and left by boorish tourists.

"I read something by a guy named Lovelock that says everything on the planet is just right for life, and that we shouldn't mess with it. That the planet itself is an organism."

"It's true that we should be careful about messing with it, but he makes too much of it. We don't need a new religion."

"Isn't it fragile?"

"Fragile and resilient at the same time."

"Don't you think individual existence is unique?"

"You're unique." He stopped, breathing noticeably. "Whoof." He could feel his heart pounding.

Vanessa turned back. "There are millions like me."

"Oh, I don't think so. Besides that grammatically impossible." She laughed.

"We'd better jog back while I can still make it."

Her smooth face scrunched in alarm. " Are you all right?"

"I'm fine. I'm just not as young as I used to be. I wish I were."

"You'd give up experience and wisdom to be young?"

"I'd like to be young and keep my experience. I guess that's a contradiction. And wisdom, if that's what it is. Knowledge and wisdom are not the same."

Was he wise? He was still himself, grown older. Aware of youth in Vanessa running easily alongside him.

"Aren't you religious at all?" she said as they reached the car.

His heart had eased. Vanessa buttoned a blouse over the top she had worn on the beach. Her mind seemed to jump without bothering about connections. He liked that in her.

He adjusted the car's air-conditioning. "If you mean do I have reverence for things, I do. I'm in awe of the marvelous adaptability of life. I felt reverence the first time I saw the Acropolis. I venerate Bach. I revere the Constitution. If you mean traditional religion, alas no. But I understand how some people find comfort in their beliefs. As the English philosopher Roger Scrutin remarks, the solace of imaginary things is not imaginary solace."

"Did you ever believe in God?"

"As I kid, I was bored with Sunday School. I thought what we had to read and what we heard was weird, like the unreal world of children's books. When I studied biology, I recognized that what we read in Sunday School was myths, the lore that preceded scientific knowledge."

"Don't you believe in progress? Isn't that evolution?"

"No. Evolution is about cells surviving, replicating themselves, mutating. There is no steady upward climb. Change occurs irregularly. Jay Gould calls it 'punctuated equilibrium.'"

"But people keep trying to rise above themselves, don't they?"

She was not afraid of engaging the pedant on his own ground. He was tempted to smile at her, but he knew that her question reflected her own struggle. "When we try to rise above our conditions, we're trying to survive."

"You're telling me that if I like you and sympathize with your feelings about your son and bring you information about him that might help explain things, that that's my instinct for survival?"

"I'm very grateful to you, and I think you are a wonderful person. We need each other to cope with our circumstances as best we can. Helping each other is part of that. And cultivating and enjoying the achievements of our cultural evolution helps us too: art, music, language, Homer, Aristotle, Confucius, Shakespeare, Donne, Bach, Mozart, Matisse, the telescope, democracy, novels, the Internet."

"Novels, the Internet? Now I know you're kidding me. But I'm glad you like me. If you're not kidding when you say that, too. My dissertation on the novel, if I ever complete it, will be the biggest boost for my survival."

"I hope I get to read it."

She shook her head with a smile. They went to their showers. When he emerged, he heard her hair dryer going. He descended to the kitchen and poured orange juice, put on bacon and eggs and slipped bread into the toaster.

"That smells good." Vanessa stood beside him and kissed him on the cheek. "Now I can say good morning," she said.

He lifted the eggs and bacon from their pans and placed them on plates. The toast popped up. "Real butter," he said.

"Hooray," she said, and buttered the toast.

"And hot water for tea," he said.

She poured steaming water over tea bags and turned off the burner. They sat at the table he had cleared of newspapers.

"God bless our food," Vanessa said.

"I apologize for being so pedantic and negative. I've gotten unused to a ordinary things. Janice used to pray before eating. I suppose we can be grateful for eggs and bacon, and especially tea," he said, sipping carefully.

"Amen," she said.

He laughed.

"I'm not taking notes," she said. "But I'm learning things. Mostly about you. What did you do when you were a kid in Wisconsin?"

"I played baseball and went hunting and fishing with my grandfather."

"You killed little animals?"

"I did when I was a kid. And deer. Stags. I remember the first deer hunt because we came on a doe that had been shot illegally and left to die. My grandfather had to finish her off. It had to be done, but I was very sad seeing her up close, her eyes especially. I gave up hunting and fishing because of Mark. He was profoundly opposed to killing any kind of animal for sport."

The memory caught him. It had been Noah who roused Mark's feelings about animals and plants. Had he seen himself as a wounded animal? Like Noah, he had taken part in nature by an act of will. But wasn't it a contradiction that he had killed himself?

Vanessa, watching him, was aware of his distraction. "I'm sorry," he said.

"I understand. Is Zinctown a real name?"

"The ground underneath the town is honeycombed with mines. But southwestern Wisconsin is beautiful."

She had not been many places, and never in Wisconsin. She longed to travel, especially to Europe.

He suggested, lightheartedly, that it was time for him to go back to Europe. Maybe they could go together, after, that is, she finished her dissertation and he his seminal paper on scientific ethics.

Her quick smile again. She touched his hand. "That would be wonderful. My company might pall after a while."

"I don't believe it."

She agreed, after he urged her, to stay another day, and he called his travel agent. He showed her the renovated buildings along the Strand, Elissa, the old steel sailing vessel, the university, art galleries. They went to La Mixteca and had Mexican food for lunch and then to the aquarium and tropical gardens at the Moody Gardens resort.

"There's a lot more to this place than I would ever have guessed. You should hire out as a tourist guide."

"Maybe I will when I retire."

"Are you going to retire?"

"I could now, I guess. Five more years and I have to."

"It seems unfair. You could quit now and help me write my dissertation."

"I'm not competent to write about novels."

"You could bring your science to bear. You're taking on the theologists and humanists about ethics, why not take on the literary gurus and novels? Saul Bellow says characters in novels are trying to master their experience. Aren't scientists like characters in novels, trying to master their discoveries and invent order?"

She was challenging him again. "*Invent* order? We do devise theories and use them as new tools. Mastery? Perhaps. But for me science is learning. What the Greeks called *paedeia*. Learning is an end in itself. Learning about the origins and development of life is the most exciting thing I do, or can imagine doing. And, as a scholar, you are drawn, despite distractions, to learning about novels, aren't you? I would like to learn what you have learned. I'm not savvy enough about literature to help you write it. But I want to read your thesis when you have it completed."

"Oh, no," she said. "I don't want you to see how badly I write."

"I don't believe you write badly. Your writing has to be as bright and articulate as you are verbally. In any case, I'll be biased."

"You are a true friend. I hope I can live up to your opinion of me." She stood up. "If you don't mind, I'd like to walk on the seawall by myself for a while. Besides I'm keeping you from your work."

"I understand. Don't feed the gulls. They quickly become pests." I'm boring, he thought. He went to the kitchen for a Boddingtons. Probably his whole project was bootless. How much of his attitude toward the assumptions of ethicists was an inversion of the irrational fundamentalism of his childhood brainwashing? How did one escape from memories of being beaten with a razor strop for a violation of a father's religion?

How did you gain freedom from dogmatic ignorance without dragging the ash pit of your past along with you? Was his preoccupation with scientific ethics as emotionally driven as Mark's obsession with injustice? Had his history disabled his objectivity? Mark had grown up free of a father's closed-minded harassments, in material plenty, with open opportunities. His environment had been identical to Jimmy's and Laurie's. Had there been a quirk in his genetic makeup, an inborn vision of how the world ought to be that his experience betrayed, that compelled his rejection of it? His suicide had been an accusation. His eyes were drawn to the box resting on a table near the door: Mark's ashes waiting, alive in him until he himself died.

His life was narrowing down toward zilch. Did his passion for the truth about ethics separate him from his true interests? Henry had implied that his ideas were irrelevant. He admired Vanessa in her struggle to fashion the self she was determined to be. Had his daughter been more inclined toward intellectual matters, she might have been like Vanessa. Had life been too easy for Laurie?

In the evening they went to the ninth floor of the Moody Hotel to Shearn's Restaurant, overlooking the west end of the island and the Gulf. They watched the sunset over the water. He ordered champagne.

"To celebrate," he said.

"What? she said.

"Our friendship," he said.

"May it survive," she said. And they laughed.

They sipped the champagne and made small talk as darkness climbed slowly from the Gulf into a rose-tinted sky and lights came on in houses and condominiums the length of the island.

29 *VANESSA PARSONS*

The distant surface of Texas moved slowly east, monotonous, and seemingly endless. She was glad to be flying back to her beloved eucalyptus trees, the dry cool air, the icy, blue Pacific. She had almost begun to take them for granted. When she got her degree, she would have to leave them for God knows where, but she would be on her own in a world remote from the ghetto.

Her days with Michael had overcome her resentment at being trapped in Mark's vengeance. Michael seemed genuinely to want to be a friend. He had treated her as a junior colleague. He had treated her as a father might have, had she been so lucky. She wanted to be an academic like him - but in her own way, and in a field and with beliefs as far from his as she could imagine. He seemed truly sad when they said goodbye.

His career was almost over. His single-mind devotion to science, his odd but determined attempt to bring it to bear on ethics - however that could be done - would probably end as an obscure footnote to the history of his discoveries. And she had no idea what those were. Her recollection of his pain at his son's life and death, of his humanity through it all, would stay with her.

What would her own career come to? Would it amount to anything more than a footnote to the unwritten history of an obscure family from another Los Angeles ghetto? Her love affair with books that began with her mother's indiscriminate reading, and passed on to her as a child, had been the motivation for her learning, and now would be the basis of her teaching and writing. Would it matter?

She would find a job. And see. When she was very young and longed for something deeply, she would say to herself, please, God. And now what she had worked for so long was within her sight. Please, God, she said quietly. She leaned her head against the cool window and fell asleep.

30 *JOSÉ VIDA*

They made them get on the bus, then they locked the door.

He did not know what he would do in Tijuana. He had never been there. That was not where he and Lupe had come over. Lupe would not know what happened to him. He worried about Juanito. They were working in the field when the *migras* came. He ran to hide in the irrigation ditch but they caught him.

He had to come back. He would cross where they crossed before and take the same route. He would stop again at the shed where his son was born. Would there be food and water? He wondered about the man who killed himself. He crossed himself. He wondered about the kind old man who gave them food and money and let them stay in the house. Would there be someone else there now? They left after the police came and took a paper from the door.

He didn't want to keep running and hiding and taking money from anyone. He was a good worker. But there was no work in his village.

They let them off at the border and they crossed into Mexico. He would go back. Where else was there besides America?

There had to be some place on God's earth for his family.

31 *MICHAEL HORNE*

The boat leaned easily against the water. Handling the ropes and sails of the rented crafty seemed odd at first, but he had not lost his skill. As he left the bay, the channel gave a different feel to the to the motion of the boat. A tanker left a rolling wave in its wake. The Gulf was calm, and an offshore breeze pushed him into gentle swells. A shrimper crossed his bow slowly, trawling. Oil platforms rose from the bright water into view as he tacked and paralleled the shore. The tall insurance building stood like a sentinel on the horizon of the island. It was half a continent away that he had taught Mark to sail.

He took the box from under his legs where he had secured it against the movement of the boat. He felt a need to say something. He remembered his pilgrimages to Noah's grave in the high desert. He opened the box and shook it to leeward until it was empty. *Vale filius.* The sound of his voice mingled with the hoarse cries of gulls that circled above the mast.

As he brought the boat about, the sails cracked and a gust of wind sprayed salt water across the deck and over his face.